Table of Contents

A Twinge of Terror

16 Light Horror Stories
Presented by
The Butchered Writers

Virefire Publishing

Cover design by: Raven Tomes

Edited by: Nora B. Peevy and Raven Tomes.

Published by: Virefire Publishing

Library of Congress Control Number: 2018675309

Dedication

Sometimes horror tiptoes on silent feet. It's not always a loud thud in the night. These are the stories for the readers who appreciate quiet horror, so sit back and curl up with your favorite cozy blanket and drink because you're in for a treat. This tome contains sixteen tales of spine-tingling terror guaranteed to give you just a "twinge" of terror before bedtime. But you might want to look underneath the bed before you go to sleep and make sure we're not still lurking there. Just in case.

Where it begins...

(Foreword)

The shadow in the dark hallway. The eyes watching from the open closet door. The hands waiting to grab you from under the bed. You've felt this kind of fear before, but you've forgotten it. Stories in this anthology aren't meant to overwhelm you with blood and gore or reinvent the wheel. "A Twinge of Terror" is here to remind you where your fear has been hiding. It's been waiting quietly, patiently, and so much closer than you remember.

Tapped In

By Melinda Pouncey

It was literally the last thing she expected to see.

When Wanda stepped out of her house to go to work, she encountered a scene of carnage she could barely imagine. Her lupins, the flowers she lovingly planted in pots on either side of her front door a couple of weeks ago, were scattered all over her walkway and yard, ripped apart stem by stem. The beautiful pink and purple blossoms littered the ground like so much trampled confetti. Wanda's hand flew to her mouth in shock and her eyes scanned the neighborhood for any sign of the culprit. What monster would do something so horrible to a bunch of innocent flowers?

She heard a magpie call nearby and her grief turned to anger. Those wretched birds! They were the ones to blame. She knew it was improbable. There were magpies in her garden often and they had never attacked her flowers before. Still, if they would kill innocent song birds, they were capable of violence toward innocent flowers. With a heavy heart, she swept up the broken stems and petals, relegating them to the trash bin before leaving for her job at the hospital.

All day the sadness clung to her as she entered patient information into the computer, discussed insurance, and reassured nervous people checking into the hospital for various maladies. She tried to ignore the feeling. It was only a few flowers after all, easily replaced, but she couldn't fully get it out of her mind. The walkway looked so drab, and without the pop of color, her front stoop was just an ordinary front stoop.

What bothered her most, aside from the flowers, was having no clear culprit to blame or guard against should she try again. If it was the magpies or some other animal, it was an annoyance, if it was a neighbor or stranger, that put a more sinister spin on the incident. She flipped through her mental index card of people she knew but came up with no one likely to have done such a heinous act. A quick backtrack of the past few days turned up no stranger she noticed that seemed out of place or hostile. In the end, she had to give up her musings and go to bed.

The next day stirred another pang of melancholy as she headed off to work, knowing they wouldn't be there to greet her when she got home. But once at work, there was no time to dwell on the flowers. They were short staffed again and she spent the day working without a break until quitting time. She walked home from the bus stop with nothing on her mind but a quick meal and a little television before bed.

She made the turn onto her walkway and as she approached the house a shiver ran up her spine. On the front stoop lay a dead magpie. The poor creature was savaged to the point that it took her a moment to identify what type of bird it was. Her bad feelings toward the magpies in her garden disappeared as she saw the feathers tumble over the lawn, fluttering in the evening breeze. Blood stained the walkway, and the head of the unfortunate bird lay next to one of the planters, its lifeless beady eye staring sightless and accusing, as though it knew she suspected it of foul deeds.

With no small measure of disgust, she disposed of the dead bird and washed the blood from the walkway. She thought about knocking on a few of her neighbors' doors and asking if they or their doorbell cameras had caught anything, but decided not to bother. It was getting dark and she didn't want people to think she was a weirdo. She'd call Marian and Jennifer after supper. If they couldn't help her, she would widen her inquiries at the weekend.

After a quick look around her darkening yard and seeing nothing out of the ordinary, Wanda shrugged and went inside. She didn't notice the bell-shaped growths erupting from a series of ropy vines threading through the nearby bushes.

That night she woke up abruptly without knowing why.

For a few moments she lay in the dark, listening to the silence of the night. A light, scraping sound against her bedroom window reassured her. Sometimes the wind made the branches of the tree move against the glass, a perfectly normal sound. She snuggled back in bed and closed her eyes with a sigh. The recent events must have affected her more deeply than she'd realized.

Just as she was about to drift off again, the sound at the window went from scraping to tapping. Her eyes shot open. Now that was unusual.

Turning her head, she could just make out the thin shadows that stretched from the tree like skeletal fingers, repeatedly striking the pane with a sound between a click and a ping. She watched in horrified fascination as the tree's finger-like twigs moved against the glass one at a time, like a person drumming their fingers rhythmically on a desk. To make things worse, there was no sound of any wind that might be creating this phenomenon.

Then the drumming stopped and the shadow moved back, curled slightly, and beckoned to her. It wasn't a mistake or trick of the light, she was certain. The twigs at the end of the branch were making a come-hither motion. Her blood ran cold. She snatched the duvet up over her head and squeezed her eyes shut.

The tapping started again in a strange pattern that reminded her of old telegraph machines she'd seen in movies. "Sending you a message. Stop. Arriving on Friday. Stop." What was that called, the thing those old machines used? She didn't remember but was too afraid to lower the covers and look at the window again. The tapping continued for a few more minutes and then abruptly stopped. She lay still a few long minutes, listening and waiting before cautiously pulling the covers down and peeking at the window. The tree branch had returned to its original position. Still, Wanda was too scared to get up and go to the window. It took another half hour for her to work up the courage to throw the covers aside, jump out of bed and run over to draw the curtains, shutting out the tree and the surrounding night.

The next morning, she pushed the duvet aside and rubbed sleep from her eyes. The memory of her dream from the night before was indistinct, but the knot in her stomach was very real as she got out of bed and began her morning routine. When she began to dress, the branch outside the window skittered across the glass, creating a shadow against the curtain. She shrieked and jumped, feeling foolish the next second.

"It's just the wind," she scolded herself, but the feeling of impending doom grew stronger instead of dissipating.

As she ate breakfast, Wanda tried scrolling her phone for tree trimming services. It was time to get rid of that rogue branch. What she had come to think of as a comforting sound before she fell asleep had become anything but, and she wasn't taking the chance of getting spooked again when the solution was so simple. At least, it would have been simple if her phone worked. Puzzled at the lack of service, she tried again and again but nothing got her a signal. She even turned the phone off and on again but it still refused to connect to the network. There had been no issues last night when she called her neighbors, though they hadn't experienced anything like what was going on at her place. Still, she'd had a couple of nice conversations that, at the time, put her at ease a little. One of them said she'd seen a stray cat in the neighborhood the previous week and to Wanda's mind the case was closed.

A cat explained both of her incidents perfectly. After the tree trimmers, she'd planned to call animal control but, apparently, she wasn't calling anyone. Not this morning anyway.

Her thoughts went to the dream again. It had to be a dream; there was no other explanation. Tiredness, stress, always the ingredients for a nightmare, and that's all it had been, she was convinced of that.

Wanda opened her door with a slight sense of foreboding that turned into full blown terror when she saw the vines. Like a macabre parody of Sleeping Beauty, thick vines covered her yard, twining and twisting over themselves, creating an impenetrable barrier she could barely make out daylight through. She ran back in the house and through to the back yard to see the same result. The vines grew in such a way as to encase her house and yard in a viney bubble. All along the vines were dark green, bell-shaped growths that hung down from them on slender stems, swaying hypnotically back and forth. A hedgehog ambled from a bush near the back fence and one of the bells descended over it, then lifted.

The hedgehog was gone, but Wanda could see the struggle inside as the bell ballooned out in several places before it finally disgorged the remains of the poor creature upon the ground. She stood frozen in shock and disgust, still on the threshold of her house. While none of the bells looked large enough to engulf a human, there were so many, she had no doubt trying to get near the vines would result in her meeting a similar fate.

She stepped back inside and closed the door. Her first thought was to grab her phone and she cursed under her breath when she realized that was a dead end. Turning on her computer didn't work either, not that she expected it would, but what else was there to do? She turned on the television, hoping for news. The emergency broadcast system was on every channel, droning an endless canned, "shelter in place" alert, but offering no information on the nature and duration of the emergency.

Suddenly, the tapping came again, this time on the door.

Wanda's heart raced as her dream came crashing back with the inevitable certainty it wasn't a dream after all. She put her hands over her ears but the tapping continued without pause. No way was she opening the door, yet there was something haunting, almost hypnotic, about the cadence of it, the pattern repeating again and again. A form of communication. How it was possible she had no idea, but was forced to accept the reality of it. And underlying it all was silence. No screaming or shouting came to her ears from the other houses surrounding her.

No sirens or traffic sounds of any kind filtered through the solid bubble of vines surrounding her home, only the tapping that continued without ceasing, vying with the monotone recorded voice on the television.

The pattern, that was the key. Like a telegraph that used long, short, long, short bursts to spell out a message... Morse code! That's what it was. But no one used Morse code anymore, did they?

Wanda went into her spare room and looked through the old dusty books on the shelf that had belonged to her dad. He had always been fascinated by codes and they'd even had their own system when she was a kid, a simple alphabet to number code no one knew but the two of them, or so she thought at the time. She searched the titles until she found one called "Understanding Morse Code".

A flood of relief washed over her and she took it into the dining room to pore over it.

With no modern tech to help or guide her, transferring the constant tapping at her door was painstakingly slow as she began to build the message.

B-I-L-L-I-O-N-S-A-R-E-O-N-E, it said. What did that mean?

She went slowly to the door and tapped out.

W-H-A-T-D-O-Y-O-U-W-A-N-T?

There was a brief pause, as though vines or trees or whatever all this was found itself surprised it was receiving a reply.

Then: J-O-I-N-U-S.

The idea both froze Wanda's blood and boiled it at the same time. How dare this... this thing, whatever it was, try to lure her in with such blatant lies.

H-O-W? she tapped.

O-P-E-N-T-H-E-D-O-O-R

N-E-V-E-R! she tapped furiously.

The tapping stopped.

Wanda sank into a chair, thinking of an article she'd read recently about how certain molds could communicate telepathically, of whole forests that were a single entity. Her mind's eye stretched to imagine this entity, this network of murderous vines covering the world. What happened to that hedgehog? Was it now part of the collective mind of this thing or had it merely been consumed?

What if this entity was bent on bringing all of humanity together as one, but in the most vicious way possible? Taking only the parts it could use, then throwing away the scraps. Eating and growing until all dissent was consumed and the world was forced to accept its fate.

Wanda decided then and there she wouldn't give in. She wouldn't join this thing in whatever manner it wanted her, and would not let this thing consume her without a fight. She glanced toward the kitchen where her pantry was stocked with food. She could hold for a while longer, and in that time maybe she could trick this thing, find a way to fight, to connect with other human beings, to take back the world.

She went back to the door and tapped out:

I-C-A-N-W-A-I-T.

After a brief pause came the reply:

W-E-C-A-N-W-A-I-T-T-O-O.

The Candle in the Window

By Raven Tomes

No one in Elmridge could agree on when the candle first appeared in the Harlow house window. Some said it had always been there, even when the town was still logging lanes and porch swings. Others swore it started the Fall the river flooded and knocked the old footbridge crooked. Adults said the candle was a power line reflection, a trick of headlights, a prank. Kids knew better.

Every night, just before the church bell tolled ten, a single taper burned in the second-floor gable window. Pale flame. Tall glass chimney. Heavy curtains on either side that never moved.

"Ghost tour fodder," said Nora's dad whenever tourists slowed on Birch Street to take pictures. He ran the hardware store and believed in screws and schedules, not stories. "Nobody's lived there since '73. Wind through broken panes looks like a candle if you squint."

Nora didn't squint. She watched. The candle never flickered when the wind gusted. It burned steady, like it had a job.

Harlow House sat hunched at the end of the street where the trees began, a Victorian with gray clapboards and a widow's walk like a crown that forgot what it was for. Yellow police tape had long since slumped from the porch columns. Local lore filled the gap neat as moss: a family that left in a hurry, a sealed nursery, a piano that played itself in storms. The truth was duller. The Harlows moved after a fire in the kitchen. Insurance money never reached the repairmen. Paperwork got lost between boxes and basements. And still, every night, the candle lit itself.

Halloween came early that year. Summer cracked and fell in a pile of dry leaves; October woke up mean and pretty. Nora's friends planned costumes that came with store-bought blood and plastic fangs. Nora planned to prove a point.

"We blow it out," she said, matter-of-fact, in the glow of her phone as they sat under the bleachers after practice. "It's a trick. A timer. Something with a pilot light. If we blow it out and it stays out, that's that."

"Big 'we,'" said Jax, picking grass out of his shoelaces. "Is this like the raccoon trap idea? Because I still have a scar."

"Raccoons heal," Nora said. "Egos don't." She grinned at him. "Come on. You're not scared."

"I'm not stupid," he said, and then sighed, because those were different things. "Fine. Tonight. But we leave if the piano starts playing."

Gina, who wore a rosary tucked under her team hoodie and said it wasn't superstitious if it was blessed, agreed to come on the condition that she was allowed to say I told you so. She folded a small flashlight into her sleeve and practiced the signs of the cross like stretching.

They met at nine-thirty at the corner where the street broke into gravel. The moon was a fingernail. The air bit gently at exposed wrists, the kind of cold that made you think about your bones. A moth clicked itself against the streetlight until it remembered better and drifted off toward a darker plan.

"Last chance," Jax murmured as the Harlow porch rose out of the dark. "We could still say we did and go home and drink cocoa and live to ninety."

"We'll be in and out," Nora said, though the house's silhouette made her chest feel like a stair she couldn't see the bottom of. "Up the stairs, second floor, window on the gable. Blow. Leave. Done."

The porch groaned a warning as they stepped up. Gina's flashlight painted long bones on the floorboards. The front door was warped wood and hinges that had held out for decades; it surprised no one when the lock gave with a push and a clack.

Inside smelled like long-dried smoke and apples that had once wanted to be pie. Sheet-draped furniture rose like a congregation caught mid-prayer. A staircase curled to the second floor, banister sticky with old varnish and dust. Somewhere deep in the house, a drip counted a lazy rhythm.

"See?" Nora whispered. "No ghosts. Just gravity."

But the candle was already burning upstairs.

They saw it from the foyer: a stripe of flame painted on the opposite wall by a narrow window above. It didn't flicker. It simply was.

They climbed. The stairs complained, then accepted them. The second-floor hallway felt like holding your breath in a long tunnel. Wallpaper vines curled over themselves; a door at the end had swelled shut and taken its frame hostage. On the right: the gable window, candle in a brass holder set safely on the sill, glass chimney clear as a throat.

Nora stepped toward it like a swimmer judging a cold lake. "Ready?" she asked.

"No," said Jax and Gina in unison.

Nora cupped her hands around the chimney and blew.

The flame thinned to a blue thread, bowed, and went out. Smoke rose like a word unsaid.

For a heartbeat, nothing happened.

"See?" Nora whispered, a laugh hitching in the word. "Timer, my butt. It was just a..."

The candle relit itself.

Not a match strike. Not a spark. One moment smoke; the next, a steady pale tongue of flame standing right where it had been, undisturbed by her breath, unbothered by physics.

Gina gasped a prayer that sounded sharp and small in the long hall. Jax stepped back hard into the opposite wall and left a dust angel.

Nora stared at the flame and tasted pride go sour. She blew again, harder, until her cheeks hurt. Out. Smoke. In. Fire.

"Okay," she said hoarsely. "Okay, so it's fine. It's a trick. Or the glass chimney gathers heat. Or—" She didn't believe herself enough to finish. The hairs on her arms stood up like listeners.

"Let's go," Gina said, fingers tight around her hidden rosary. "Nora. Please."

Nora wanted to agree. She wanted to laugh and say fine and mean it. But curiosity was heavier than fear. It always had been. She lifted the chimney. The flame bent but didn't shudder. She pinched the wick between forefinger and thumb. It stung like touching ice. Dark. Smoke. Light.

Jax was already halfway down the stairs. Gina hovered like a stern angel waiting to see if she needed to drag someone by the collar. "Nora," she tried again, softer now. "Whatever it's doing, maybe it's doing it for a reason."

"Because it's petty?" Nora said, but the joke missed its target. The candle's steady burn meant something; she could feel it. It felt like a clock striking in a house that had forgotten the hour.

She followed the wire of that thought down the hall to the swollen door. The one that had taken a bite out of the frame and held it. The one that didn't belong to a bedroom or a bath, to judge by where windows should have been.

"Nora," Gina warned, but Nora was already bracing a shoulder and exhaling into the push. Wood groaned. Paint cracked like a dry smile. The door opened six inches and exhaled a cold that had been waiting decades to be allowed out.

Inside: a small room lit only by the candle's spill. Shelves. Jars. A child's desk with a marble run half-built, frozen mid-course. A rocking chair with the cushion collapsed as if someone had just stood up after a very long sit. On the far wall, a square of darker wallpaper where a picture had hung.

Between the shelves, a narrow window. Not the gable one. A different one, facing the woods. Its glass was not like the other windows. This one was cloudy with age and something else, like breath caught between panes.

"What is it?" Gina asked, voice collared tight.

Nora stepped in. The floor groaned in the peculiar way floors do when they want to be careful and are too old for the effort. She raised her phone light. The jars held old preserves turned to amber stone. A label, buckled and brown, read PEARS 1969. Something had pressed small marks into the dust of the desk like tracks.

"Kid's room?" Jax asked from the hall, trying to sound bored and landing on braced.

"No bed," Nora murmured. "No toys."

"Pantry?" Gina tried.

Nora stood before the cloudy window. The old sash stuck stubborn and familiar under her fingers. She pried. It freed with a sigh and a smell like wet stone. Air came in from the woods—cold, leaf-sweet, patient.

The candle behind her fluttered and steadied.

"Listen," Jax said suddenly. "Do you hear that?"

They did. Faint at first, then not faint. A sound like water being poured slowly into something deep. Then a second sound, the click of glass on glass. Then a tiny scritch, like a matchhead against grit.

Nora turned.

In the hallway, along the baseboards, something dark seeped like tea under a door. It pooled in a thin line, then rose, not like smoke, not like fog, like ink learning to stand. It slid along the floor toward the pantry room, elegant, inevitable.

The candle flame leaned toward it and did not gutter.

Gina grabbed Nora's elbow. "We need to go."

Nora should have. She knew that like you know in dreams that you have to run and your legs are milk. But a thought had found purchase and made a home. If the candle wasn't for lighting the room, if it was steady, a job, if it relit itself because there was something it needed to keep lit, then maybe it wasn't for them at all. Maybe it was for the window. Or for what leaned against the window from the other side.

She looked at the cloudy pane and saw, just for a second, her own reflection misbehave. It moved a fraction late. Then it moved when she didn't.

"Nora," it mouthed without sound, and she felt her stomach fall, as through a trap. The word wasn't a warning. It was a rehearsal.

The ink at the threshold reached the pantry's line of light and shivered. It tasted the air. It pushed a slick edge forward and touched the candle's warm circumference. The flame lifted, quaintly, like it was ducking under a rope.

"Out," Gina said, voice breaking. "Now."

They ran. Panic made the house seem smaller, the doors less tall. Stairs tried to be too many. The foyer took a day to arrive. Jax hit the front stoop like he wanted to break it. Nora followed, then stopped at the threshold because she was her father's daughter and leaving a thing wrong made her itch.

She looked back.

The candle burned steady in the gable window. The pantry window glowed faint and cloudy, a throat trying to clear itself. The ink that was not smoke didn't cross the line of the light. It pressed its nose to it. It learned the taste of warm glass and waited, patient as weather.

Nora closed the door gently. She slid the warped lock home. She stepped back into the cold and stood with her friends in the yard under the moth-fretted streetlight. They listened. The house exhaled. The drip resumed.

"You're white as chalk," Jax said eventually. "Your freckles look like punctuation."

Nora laughed and it came out wrong. "It's not lighting the house," she said. "It's lighting the window."

Gina shivered so hard her teeth clicked. "So we keep it lit," she said. "Right? We tell someone? The fire department? The—"

"Who?" Jax said, gently this time. "Who would you tell that a ghost candle is keeping the woods from walking into a pantry?"

They walked home in the middle of the street. Every porch light on Birch suddenly looked less decorative and more like locks.

Over the next week, Nora watched the Harlow house like it owed her a piece of herself back. At ten, the candle lit. Once, a wind came howling down off the ridge and pushed at every window on the street; the flame leaned like a dancer and did not go out. Twice, a raccoon climbed the porch post and peered in the front door window with the slow astonishment of raccoons; it left again.

After the third night, Nora walked to the library. The town newspaper archive lived in gray boxes with gray tape, the kind of history that always smells like a basement no matter where you store it. She sat at a table under the hiss of the fluorescent lights and read her town backward.

She found the Harlows. A wedding announcement...lace gloves, lemon cake, a photograph of two people who looked like they would be kind to cashiers. A baby announcement. Another. A column about a kitchen fire and the way a neighbor boy had run to bang on the door until everyone came out into the yard together, coughing, laughing. Then, in 1973, a paragraph with no photo. Estate sale, contents of house at 421 Birch. Items to include: antique brass candleholders, marble games, preserves (sealed), glassware, mirror. Widow requests privacy.

Nora traced the skin-thin newsprint with her thumb. Mirror. Pantry. Preserves. Candleholder.

She checked out a book about Victorian household customs and read it under the covers by phone light. Entire chapters on mirrors draped after a death. On windows cracked open an inch so the soul could find its way. On candles kept burning to light returns.

She didn't sleep well. In her dreams, the pantry window had something on the other side, something the exact size and shape of her shadow, tapping.

She told her dad over pancakes on Saturday. He laughed and kissed the top of her head. "You're your mother," he said, which was both a compliment and a warning. "Promise me you won't go back in."

"I won't," she said automatically.

She meant it when she said it.

On Sunday, just before ten, the candle didn't light.

Nora was already in her coat before she realized she was moving. Her dad was on the phone with a supplier and waved as she slipped out, assuming library or Gina or both. The night felt wrong. Too open. Streetlights hummed the way they do when they're thinking of going out.

At the Harlow fence, Jax appeared at her shoulder like a loyal curse. "You weren't going without me," he panted.

"Gina?" Nora asked.

"Mass," he said. "She texted, all caps. I think she's praying on the move."

They climbed the porch. The door sulked and let them in. The house felt awake. The drip had stopped, which was somehow worse.

Upstairs, the gable window was a dark coin. The pantry door gaped a little wider, like a mouth practicing.

Nora ran.

Inside the pantry, the cloudy window was clearer than she remembered. Something had polished the inner pane with long, patient strokes. A handprint bloomed briefly, childish-small and then not small, on the glass.

The candle on the gable sill sat unlit, wick blackened and confident. Nora's hands shook as she struck a kitchen match from the box she had brought and lowered it to the wick. The match hissed. A small obedient flame rose, the size of a question mark.

It went out.

"Come on," Nora whispered. She lit another. Out. Another. Out. Each time the pantry window brightened, eager. Each time the flame died.

"Nora," Jax said, voice small in the hall. "It doesn't want to."

"It needs to," she said through her teeth. "Hold the chimney."

He did, hands careful, eyes huge. Nora cupped the match and struck it along the brass of the holder. It flared like a promise. She touched it to the wick and held her breath. The wick caught, not like before. This time the fire felt heavier, less like a pet and more like a worker reporting for duty.

The pantry window went cloudy again. The handprint faded. The room exhaled.

Nora laughed, a brief animal sound, and set the chimney back in place with the solemnity of a crown.

"You can't babysit a candle forever," Jax said as they stood at the top of the stairs, both reluctant to turn their backs on the window.

"I can tell the town," Nora said.

"And they'll laugh." He reprimanded.

"I can tell your aunt with the ghost meter."

"She's banned from my house." He reminded her solemnly, a worried glance piercing his eyes as she continued frantically.

"I can tell the fire department to do night checks." She suggested rapidly.

"They're already mad about fireworks."

"Then I'll tell the house," Nora said. "Every night. Like a chore. Like a habit."

And that's what she did.

At 9:58, she checked the wick. At 10:00, she watched it light. When it didn't, she lit it. She learned which matches were too damp and which chimneys made the flame gutter. She learned the pantry window liked to test its edges on windless nights and was lazier when it rained. She learned the sound of ink learning to stand and how to not hear it if she needed to sleep after.

She told Gina and Jax. She told no one else. The secret felt like a candle under its own glass, steady because it had to be.

Winter came early that year, and with it a power outage that wrapped the town in a blanket woven from breath. Families told each other stories in living rooms. The Harlow house's window burned like a single tooth in the dark.

Nora and Jax trudged up the porch steps with hats pulled low and matches in their pockets. Gina met them with a thermos of hot cocoa and a thin-lipped frown that meant she was braver than she wanted to be.

"You know this is ridiculous," Jax muttered as Nora checked the wick with gloved fingers.

"Yup," Nora said, and smiled with her head down so the house wouldn't see it and get cocky.

The candle took light easily that night. The pantry window, polite, fogged over like a mirror with no one looking. Beyond it, the trees moved without going anywhere.

"Who's going to do this when you go to college," Jax said lightly. "Hire a kid? Start a club? Candle Corps?"

Nora's throat tightened with a future that suddenly had a hinge. "Teach me to set a timer that works on ghosts," she said.

"You think your dad will ever believe you?" Gina asked.

"No," Nora said. "But he'll install a smoke detector."

They laughed. The house listened and didn't mind. The candle burned without wavering. Somewhere on Birch Street a generator barked awake; elsewhere a neighbor opened a door and let the cold learn the layout of a kitchen. The town went on being a town because most of the time that's what towns do.

In the spring, tourists returned in their sensible shoes. The ghost tour brochure added a new bullet under Harlow House: Candle rumored to light nightly. Do not trespass. Photos appeared on feeds with filters that made the sky bruise purple. Comments threaded into arguments about what was real.

Nora didn't comment. She carried a book of matches in her pocket the way some people carry talismans. If she had to leave town someday, she would teach someone else the habit. It would be boring and holy. It would be easy until it wasn't, and then easy again.

On the last night of school, the three of them stood in the yard with the moths and the streetlight and watched the candle through the gable window while the pantry window stayed cloudy and content. Jax nudged her with his shoulder.

"You ever going to tell me what you saw in the glass," he asked softly, "that first night?"

Nora watched the flame stand its small watch. "No," she said, kindly. "But I'll keep the light on for it."

The house said nothing. The woods listened. The candle burned, and the town slept, and the thing on the other side learned patience all over again.

Some lights are for seeing. Some are for keeping. You don't always get to decide which kind you're in charge of.

But if you're lucky, somebody shows up with matches.

A Gilded Butterfly

By Glynn Owen Barras

"Beware the Jabberwock, my son!
The jaws that bite, the claws that catch!"
~Lewis Carroll, Jabberwocky

"Vacancies," the card behind the fly-spotted window stated. The house stood tall and narrow, squeezed tightly between its neighbors. Elanor, discouraged by the dirty windows and the peeling paint, had almost ignored this one. But her walk had been long. The suitcase, holding all her worldly possessions, felt heavy, and her feet ached considerably.

So, standing before a door spotted with peeling black paint, (leprous was the word she'd use), Elanor deposited her case to the floor.

I have a bad feeling about this. This thought was nothing new. She'd experienced nothing but bad feelings for months, ever since the turn of 1927 and her decision to escape her abusive husband. Raising her hand, she reached for a brass knocker shaped like a lion's head, and knocked. Three sharp raps. No answer.

Should I?

Three sharp raps further, and one for good luck.

Nothing. She retrieved her case and turned back to the street. The noise of bolts sliding open made her pause.

In for a penny, Elanor thought, turning back to the door. It creaked open, and her hesitation swelled.

♦♦♦

"So what brought you to Kingsport?"

The elderly woman interviewing her had probably never been pretty, even in her youth. She wore a black dress, white frills at the collar and cuffs. Add this to the severe grey-haired bun, she resembled a widow in mourning. A large tabby cat sat watching Elanor from her lap. He wasn't the only one. Other cats stared at her from atop cabinets and chairs.

"Mrs.... "

"You may call me Mrs. Scott Glancy."

"Mrs. Scott Glancy," Elanor repeated. "I fancied a break from the big city, Boston that is, and my family came from here originally."

"Oh?" Mrs. Scott Glancy's eyes widened at this. "Your surname, my dear?"

"Walcott," Elanor replied, using her maiden name.

"Oh, I have met many Walcotts over the years." Mrs. Scott Glancy smiled. "Are you any relation to the Arkham Walcotts?"

Elanor shook her head and relaxed a little further into the well stuffed, slightly threadbare seat.

"Not that I know of, but it's possible."

Mrs. Scott Glancy nodded, a slight smile forming on her lips. It appeared she'd come to a decision. Elanor's earlier reservations were dissipating. She felt better, better anyway than when the stern-faced, heavily wrinkled beldam had answered the door and led her to this dark, dusty room filled with cats.

"Well my dear, you are welcome to stay."

Relief flooded her body. After everything she'd been through, Elanor counted this as a win.

"I have quite a motley array of tenants," Mrs. Scott Glancy continued. "They include a Spiritualist – Ms. Rawlings, a woman quite famous at the turn of the century. She has visitors here on occasion, for seances. There are three gentlemen: a deeply religious German called Hans Glanz, a polite young man named Mr. Smith, I never see him at meals, and Howard Phillips. He is a writer, or so he claims. Your room is located beneath his garret. If his typewriter gets too much for you in the night, let me know, and I will have words."

Elanor considered this. The last thing she needed was to be on bad terms with a long-standing tenant.

"It'll be fine I'm sure."

"Your rent is three dollars a week, which includes breakfast and an evening meal."

Elanor nodded. With her cash reserves, this appeared quite reasonable.

"Two weeks in advance." Mrs. Scott Glancy paused, pursing her lips. Could this be the final test?

"Of course. I'll give you it now." Elanor leaned forward, reaching for her handbag.

Mrs. Scott Glancy's face beamed with approval.

Elanor delved into her purse, counted the cash, and passed it over.

Mrs. Scott Glancy tucked the notes into her dress and began to get up. The perturbed cat leapt from her lap to scurry off into the shadows.

"Follow me, dear," she said, and proceeded to escort Elanor from the room.

Beyond the door stood a narrow lobby and a narrower staircase. A frayed tortoiseshell carpet covered both floor and steps. It went well with the peeling beige wallpaper.

The house looked a cramped place, a little claustrophobic even. Elanor's life had been claustrophobic for so long now, what did it matter?

Mrs. Scott Glancy ascended, her dress bustling against the wall and banister. Elanor followed slowly, heaving her suitcase at a discreet distance. As they passed the second floor, she heard music issuing from somewhere.

"The Spiritualist and the German are on this floor," Mrs. Scott Glancy said on passing. Soon after, they reached the third floor.

"Here we are." Mrs. Scott Glancy departed the stairs and entered a short lobby, dimly lit by a small window at its termination. Halfway along the lobby two black doors faced one another. The walls and ceiling were green, while underfoot lay a Turkish Rug that had witnessed better days, weeks, and decades. She led Elanor towards the door on the right.

"I hope you enjoy your stay here, my dear. If you need anything, I am just downstairs." Mrs. Scott Glancy reached the door, opened it and pointed inside.

"Thank you," Elanor replied, smiled, and entered her new home. Mrs. Scott Glancy patted her on the shoulder and departed the way she'd come.

The room had a frayed green carpet, a white ceiling, and beige walls with a faded pattern. It appeared clean, at least. The furniture consisted of a bed, a dressing table, and a chair. A small trunk stood at the foot of the bed.

Elanor placed her case atop the trunk and headed towards the room's single window. A door to the bed's left led to the bathroom, probably, unless the house had a communal. She would check on this in a little while.

The curtains were thin, the yellow material patterned with flowers. Dust coated the glass beyond. Elanor parted the curtains and examined the view.

The street below was cobbled, the sidewalks leading to tall, narrow houses. The gable ends of their rooftops held small, circular windows. Clusters of chimney pots arrayed the roofs, many pumping smoke into an already cloudy sky. Beyond the smoke, she discerned the hint of a hilltop.

Kingsport was surrounded by hills, the very earth it was built upon uneven and bumpy. When she first departed the train station, Elanor had encountered huge, gambrel-roofed houses mounted upon the uneven land. All private residences, none held rooms to rent. Descending the hilly terrain, she'd headed into the city proper, entering its narrow, twisting lanes. Her explorations taking her close to the docks, she'd smelled salt in the air, and heard the distant bells of buoys.

Then she came across Kane Street, a little wider than the serpentine streets she'd already traversed, and less ... gloomy? Certainly, the shadow that had trailed her from Boston dissipated somewhat. And now, a new life and a new beginning were in her grasp. Here's hoping.

Elanor turned from the window and approached her suitcase. Brown fabric with rusted metal corners, it looked old, well-used, a little battered. Story of my life, she thought, and opened it.

She scanned the contents. Mostly clothes, shoes, and some toiletries, these were her sole belongings. A little miserable really. Shaking her head, she reached for the zippered pocket beneath the lid. The pocket held underwear and her lifeline: a large brown envelope. She retrieved it and held it to her chest.

Elanor stepped around to the bed and emptied the envelope's contents onto the wash-worn bedsheet. A bundle of dogeared notes and two small envelopes spilled out. It was all the cash she owned, apart from the coins and dollar bills in her purse. Fifty five dollars in total, it might have to last a long time, depending on how quickly she found a job, and, if she stayed. The white envelope held her references, one from the school she'd briefly worked at, the other from her secretarial job.

I'll do anything I can get, if it keeps a roof over my head.

The other, brown envelope held her marriage and birth certificates.

Bastard, Elanor thought, thinking of the former. She should just burn it. But for some reason, she didn't have the heart to.

Well. She retrieved the envelopes, placing them in her handbag. Taking a ten dollar bill from the cash, she replaced the remainder in the large envelope. Then she returned it to her suitcase.

I should rest, I really should, Elanor thought, but she wanted to get something done about her work position. *I still have my coat and hat on anyway, might as well get it over with.*

With this in mind, she pocketed the ten dollar bill and headed to the door, closed it behind her, and stepped into the lobby. Walking towards the stairs, she heard heavy footsteps, puffing and panting, and encountered the one making the noise.

The man was of medium height, wide and portly. Dressed in a brown wool suit, he had half a dozen books under one arm. His round face bore a sheen of sweat, his balding blonde head bearing a poor combover. He looked surprised to see her, but a quick smile turned his face jolly.

"Oh. Oh hello, Miss." He fumbled with his books and juggled them two-handed for a moment before tucking them under the other arm. "Are you the new tenant?"

"Um ... Elanor Walcott. I just moved in." She held out her hand. The man took it. She noticed ink stains on his fingers. *The writer then?*

He nodded quickly and shook her hand in a gentle grip. He cleared his throat so loudly, the noise echoed through the staircase.

"Elanor. That comes from the Hebrew you know? 'El' meaning 'god,' and 'or' meaning 'light.' Your name quite literally means 'God is my light,' or 'God is my candle.' Very pretty."

"Oh, thank you." Elanor found herself blushing.

"Oh. Erm. My name is Howard Phillips." He performed a short bow. "At your service Miss Walcott."

She smiled. What a kind man.

"If there's anything you need, give me a knock." He pointed upwards. "I'm just upstairs."

♦♦♦

The waiter serving her wore a sparkling white apron to match his sparkling white smile. He left the coffee jug on her table along with a bowl of sugar. Today, Elanor wanted her coffee black, thick with sweetness. Her coat was slung behind her chair, her hat sitting on the seat beside her.

The checkered yellow and white tabletop held the ghosts of coffee rings. Her pocketbook, opened to a page of notes, sat beside her mug. She took a sip of joe and slumped back into her seat.

A few hours of Kingsport had led to two conclusions. One: finding a job wouldn't be easy; and two: her feet needed a day's rest. The latter was due to the city's clumsy layout. As she'd witnessed on arrival, the hilly terrain hardly gave Kingsport a level spot to walk on. Everything was stacked haphazardly, from the homes and businesses, to the churches flanked by dark, sprawling graveyards.

Winding streets descended to dark cul-de-sacs, or rose towards steep hills. This diner though was near the docks, and built upon flatter ground. Empty, apart from her and the young waiter, noises issued from a kitchen beyond the counter. She'd removed her shoes, her stockinged feet cooling on the linoleum floor.

Elanor took another acrid, sugary drink, and looked out the window. The view boasted a row of three-storied houses, crumbling with age. This contrasted with the clean, new-looking diner surrounding her. This was something she'd noticed about Kingsport: its buildings were a stark mixture of the old and the new. Wooden steps between two of the houses descended to the beach. She would see the ocean if she stood up. If she weren't so tired, she'd take a walk there. Maybe another day.

She turned her attention to the pocketbook and ran her finger down the penciled notes. They were few and sparse. During her rounds she'd encountered no colleges and only one school, the most modern-looking building in Kingsport. The receptionist there had advised her to contact The Massachusetts Department of Education, for they allocated teaching posts. Not a complete bust, she'd just have to send a résumé and hope for the best. Perhaps Howard Phillips would type some extra copies up? The Kingsport Chronicle and The Kingsport Historical Society, the two other places she'd tried, held no job vacancies. She still had the courthouse and The Kingsport Public Library to check out, however, but not today. Staff at the newspaper told her some vacancies might open up later in the year. She'd drop a résumé off there, for the future.

Future. Now there's a thing. Is Kingsport the right place to be? There'd been other options, Arkham, for example, but Kingsport had appealed to her more. Considering Boston stood less than twenty miles away, she'd hardly ever heard Kingsport mentioned. This was good, if she could just—

The bell above the entrance tinkled. Two men bustled in, fishermen, by their attire. Both had faces weathered by the elements. One strode straight to the counter, the other noted her and smiled politely.

"Hey Bill, Cody," the waiter said, "the usual?"

"Please," a gruff voice replied, and she watched the fishermen get into their seats.

She returned her attention to her notebook. A moment later, the waiter reappeared at her table.

"I need this," he explained, reaching for the coffee pot. "I'll bring you a fresh one in just a tic."

He retrieved the coffee pot, and pausing, examined her notes. "Having any luck?" Perhaps she wasn't the first person he'd served here after a futile search for work.

"Ah, no," she replied. "I'm gonna try again tomorrow. Some of the smaller businesses maybe."

"Hmmm yeah," he nodded understandingly. "You might have better luck on harborside. Though ..." he put the coffeepot back on the table and rubbed his chin. "We could probably use someone here for the morning shift, Miss?"

"Walcott," she replied, "and I have references!"

◆◆◆

Today ended Elanor's fifth day of employment. She had the morning shift as the waiter, Teddy, short for Theodore, promised. Five early starts and finishes, from 8 a.m. to 1 p.m., the last of which she walked home from through Kingsport's streets.

Due to its proximity to the ocean, Kingsport mornings were incredibly foggy. Every day she descended streets carpeted in mist, the winding, labyrinthine paths, diaphanous white in the distance. It felt like she headed towards some mysterious fairyland, another realm.

These flights of whimsy had grown during her time in Kingsport. Never of a poetic bent, something about the place brought out the ethereal in her. Her chilly morning journeys led to docks so thick with mist that the ship masts appeared to emerge from nothingness. Bells and buoys rang from the ether with gentle, numbed tones. Then there was the house, the one atop the cliffs of Kingsport Point, north of the city. Elanor sometimes thought she saw lights in the grey-peaked dwelling, but from the distance she couldn't be sure.

Waitressing hardly tasked her. Taking orders, delivering coffee to mostly quiet, taciturn fishermen. At lunchtime, she served the lively, enthusiastic people from the artist colony in Hilltown. It would cover her rent and then some.

Still, the job could be a little tiring to someone unused to being on their feet, so, as Elanor turned the corner onto Kane Street she anticipated her bed.

She froze. Kingsport had very few automobiles. She'd only witnessed two downtown, and heard one in the night. But there it sat, parked across from her lodgings. The bright blue vehicle looked out of place on a street of monochrome colors.

Elanor composed herself and continued walking. As she neared she saw the plates. Boston plates. My god. She went weak at the knees and found herself, without conscious volition, speeding her gait towards home.

Two shadowy silhouettes sat in the front seats. The glowing cherry of a cigarette end appeared near the one on the driver's side, followed by a puff of smoke from the window.

Elanor ran now, the sound of her heels heavy on the sidewalk. Any moment she expected the car door to open, the hated, evil form of her husband stepping to the cobbles with malicious intent. Paranoia, that's all this is. Look at how well you covered your tracks. She was a dozen yards from Mrs. Scott Glancy's now.

He knows I'm Boston, born and bred. He doesn't know I have ancestors here. Why would he even come here?

Elanor entered the yard fronting the house. Reaching the door seconds later, thankfully, it was unlocked. Darting inside, she slammed the door, her sweating hands gripped around the doorknob. Her heart pounded and her breaths came fast and urgent.

Paranoid.

Is that a car door opening?

Just a coincidence.

Footsteps?

Elanor backed away through the lobby, her steps leaden. At any moment, she expected the door to burst open. It didn't, and after waiting some minutes longer, her breathing slowed and her jackhammer heart ceased beating so strongly in her chest.

The fear and apprehension left her as weak as a kitten. Mounting the stairs, she ascended like an invalid, using bannisters for support and feeling she might fall at any moment. After unlocking her door, Elanor found a reserve of strength and used it to hurry to the window. The car was gone.

A tap on her door made her wince. Oh. Who could that be? Not someone from the car surely? Elanor slipped out of her heels and tiptoed towards the door. She took a deep breath. "Who is it?"

Silence for a little while, then a female voice, muffled by the wooden barrier. "I am your downstairs neighbor."

The spiritualist? Elanor opened the door a crack. A diminutive woman stood there waiting. Ms. Rawlings. A strong, spicy odor surrounded her. Very pungent, exotic even. She wore a green coat and a black velvet hat covered in tatty yellow feathers. Dark tinted glasses concealed much of her face, the visible skin pale. Relieved she was her visitor, Elanor opened the door fully.

"Hello young lady." Even with the door open, her voice sounded muted. "I am Ms. Rawlings from downstairs. And you are?" The woman's elfin face broke into a smile of tiny brown teeth. *Nosey, or overly polite?*

"I'm Elanor, here for a vacation," she lied, offering her hand.

Ms. Rawlings hand was small, knobby with arthritis. It felt icy cold in Elanor's grip. They shook, and Ms. Rawlings continued. "I wanted to say hello, and also ... on occasion, I have guests come to my room. Tomorrow night is such an occasion. I apologize in advance for any disturbances you hear."

"Oh that's alright. I usually sleep like a log."

Ms. Rawlings chuckled, revealing the brown-toothed smile again. "Gods bless you, dear." At this, she shuffled off towards the stairs.

◆◆◆

I usually sleep like a log. The second night after seeing the car, Elanor still had trouble sleeping. No other incidents had occurred. Still the fear remained. How long would it take to pass? Not long, she hoped.

Tonight, like the night before, she stared at the ceiling and tried to force herself to sleep. A couple of mystery novels sat on the bedside table, borrowed from Howard Phillips, but she was too tired to read, too wired to sleep. Rain had begun falling earlier. Much heavier now, it slashed against the window.

This wasn't the only sound. In the room above, Howard Philips worked diligently at his typewriter. Some noises had issued from below earlier, shifting furniture and muttering voices. The room was silent now. Or the noise was inaudible because of the rain.

Again she tried clearing her head. Difficult, with the niggling doubts, itching at her like a rash. Nevertheless, having avoided the usual nap after her morning shift, the fatigue crept closer. Before Elanor knew it, she'd fallen asleep. And then ...

The dream was a familiar one. She'd experienced it many times, long before her arrival at Kingsport. Elanor was running through a house, a house of impossible dimensions.

Each and every room led to another room. Endless. She couldn't stop running because something unseen stalked her relentlessly. Elanor's dream panic sent her hurrying forwards, for to stop... there could be no stopping. To halt was to die.

In her waking hours, it wouldn't take Freud to decipher the dream's meaning. Every time she opened a door, Elanor expected to find the thing pursuing her in wait. Tall and mighty, with biting teeth and grabbing, clawing hands. So, Elanor continued through the unending doors, through rooms she never fully witnessed in her panicked flight.

The next door opened into a black void. Surprised and unable to halt her momentum, Elanor fell through the darkness. She landed heavily on her own bed. This was unexpected. Elanor tried to move but her limbs felt leaden. A low buzz reached her ears, followed by an unexpected lurch that spun her clockwise.

One, two, three turns of the clock, and she was falling again, not as swiftly this time. Elanor felt herself pass through her bed and the floorboards. Another lurch, and she was upside down, gaining a weird, birds-eye view of the room beneath her own. *What the?*

She hovered above a table seating four people. Their hands were joined, little finger to little finger. All their eyes were closed. Directly below her sat the diminutive Ms. Rawlings. The woman's head moved in a circular motion, her glasses catching the light from a candle at the table's center. Some strange trance was upon her.

To her right sat an elderly man with white hair and beard to match. Dressed from another era, he had the collar of his frock coat pulled high around his neck.

He faced another man, this one cadaverously thin. Olive-skinned, with distinctly canine features, he had brown hair combed over a balding scalp. He wore a new-looking pinstripe suit.

The final figure sat across from Ms. Rawlings. Large and bald, his scabby head appeared green in places. His eyelids covered a pair of huge, bulging eyes. The man looked oddly muscled beneath a stained black suit.

She's with the Kingsport Elders, Elanor thought. The Terrible Old Man, The Ghoul, and The Frogman. This thought came to her unbidden.

Is this a dream? It felt real, as real as a thing like this could feel, anyway. Elanor's curiosity started to overcome her fear as she examined the silent tableau.

Beside the candle sat a large bronze egg suspended on wires inside of a wooden box. Five starfish-shaped copper bowls surrounded the box and candle. The bowls issued smoke, the same exotic smell Ms. Rawlings had about her when they'd met.

"Ohhhhhhh," Ms. Rawlings moaned. "I've found him. Now, complete the binding."

The men started chanting, a monotonous drone in a language Elanor didn't recognize. As they continued, she felt a tugging sensation in her chest. The fear returned. This dream was growing stranger, more frightening. The chant filled her ears. The tugging transformed into a powerful wrench. She felt her very essence being taken from her.

The bronze egg snapped in two. The insides sparkled and glowed red. The egg sourced the tug, its crimson depths hungering for her soul. And oddly enough, this didn't seem so bad. The more she stared at the egg, the calmer she felt. Scarlet plains awaited her there, infinite starfields in a ruby red sky. An end to pain and thought. Just ... Oblivion. *Take me.*

Ms. Rawlings jerked in her seat and looked up. The old man pointed a gnarled finger right at Elanor.

"Tis' the wrong mind we summon!" he said, his deep voice at odds with his frail appearance. "Send her away!"

Ms. Rawlings started shouting gibberish words in an odd, liquid voice. The lure of the red world disappeared. All that remained was her vulnerability at being discovered.

Elanor's body twisted around to face the ceiling. An invisible force shoved her up and through it. Darkness followed. A moment later, she was awake. Elanor felt disorientated, her body soaked in sweat.

Outside, the rain continued to pour. Above, Howard Phillips tap-tap-tapped rhythmically at his typewriter.

◆◆◆

Sleep came easily despite her strange experience. The next morning, Elanor felt quite fatigued, however, her face in the bathroom mirror wan and dark around the eyes. She washed and dressed quickly, not wanting to be late for work.

During her time at Kane Street she'd never seen her neighbor, the elusive Mr. Smith, or heard his door for that matter. Upon leaving her room, she found that door ajar. A foul odor emanated from his room, accompanied by a murmuring voice.

Elanor felt intrigued. Creeping towards Smith's door, she fought a sneeze from the smell. Pausing behind the door, she listened.

"Mount the small quartz crystal onto the Y-clamp. Yes. Adjust the mirror two to seventeen degrees. Yes. Take mirror five, turn it three degrees. Angle it to face the scryer. Load up the vibro-needles using gold solder. Invoke the Voorish Sign, then the Elder Sign, second branch ascension."

What the? Elanor backed up. Whatever he was up to in there, it was really no business of hers. The voice continued as she headed for the stairs.

Her fatigue wore off during a busy morning shift. The usually taciturn fishermen were in good spirits due to a bountiful morning catch. The tips were fantastic, and would go towards buying the gramophone she wanted. She completely forgot about last night's strange dream.

Later, Elanor returned to her lodgings with a distinct spring in her step. Stepping onto her floor, she found Mr. Smith's door still open. *I wonder if I'll meet him*, she considered absently, not caring either way.

Upon reaching her door, she inserted her key only to find it unlocked. *I must have forgotten earlier*. She stepped inside, the figure seated on her bed not registering until she closed the door behind her. Fear flushed through her like ice water.

It was her husband, Ben, his hat and coat on the bed beside him, her suitcase packed at his feet, she assumed.

"Why hello, my sweet, wandering butterfly." The predatory grin didn't reach his eyes.

The shock sent the keys tumbling from her hand. Her handbag slipped from her arm.

"How ..."

His grin widened. "My father's money of course. Private detectives at every train station in the county. I got in here after posing as a census taker, picked your lock myself."

That car the other day.

"I'll..." Elanor backed away, pressing her body against the door.

"I've packed your things. My car is round the corner." Ben stood. The action made her feel like a cornered animal.

"Come, get your case." His tone gave no options for refusal, not if she was to avoid being hit.

Ever the gentleman. You bastard. Elanor took a step forward. Her fear compelled her, like some irresistible charm controlled her movements.

Ben reached down, lifted the case two-handed, one hand at the top, one at the bottom. Their eyes met. His were leering and triumphant.

She wanted to look away, but felt entranced, fallen victim to the snake's hypnosis. Elanor went to accept the case, arms trembling. But something inside her told her to rebel.

"No!"

She shoved the case into his face, hard. His head snapped back, and he fell floundering to the bed.

Elanor released the case and heard it crash to the floor as she turned to run. Her panicked flight returned her to the lobby. Heading for the stairs, she stumbled to a halt at the sound of ascending footsteps.

Where. Where? The window? Too high. Smith's?

She dashed towards Smith's room and had the door slammed closed behind her a moment later. The room was larger than her own, with a bed beside the window and a square table at the center.

What the?

The table held a device of metal wheels and rods, magnifying glasses and concave mirrors. A man sat slumped behind it. Thin of face with lank black hair, his eyes were rolled back. She assumed he was the elusive Mr. Smith. He wore a brass helmet spotted with tiny red gems, and appeared quite dead.

Thinking to hide, Elanor hurried to and around the table. She saw Smith's hand gripped a metal switch of some sort, connected to the device on the table. The helmet was connected to the device too, by a long, delicate wire. *Has he electrocuted himself?*

The door crashed open. Ben stood within the doorframe, his face aflame with anger. Blood trickled from his nostrils, turning his blonde moustache crimson. His once pristine white shirt was spattered in red, bringing her some degree of satisfaction. He stalked forwards.

"Just what have you gotten yourself into?" he asked, revealing crimson-coated teeth. He smirked upon reaching her. Elanor was frozen to the spot. *I'm trapped. Unless ... the cap. The switch.*

He paused with the table between them. Elanor said, "Catch," and grabbing the cap tossed it towards him.

He caught it by reflex, the confusion evident on his face. Quick as a flash, Elanor reached for Smith's clenched fist. Finding the switch, she pressed it down. For a moment, nothing happened.

"You crazy cow," Ben said.

The device came alive with motion and sound. The wheels turned faster and faster. Rods pumped with life. The device thrummed, vibrating all over. It issued that odd smell she'd noted earlier.

Ben began to shake, a spastic shudder that rattled his whole body.

Elanor backed away, watched his face spasm, his teeth chatter, and his eyes disappear to the whites.

Checkmate, you bastard.

One final shudder, and he collapsed to the floor. She reached down to Smith's cold hand, waited a little longer to see if Ben moved, and switched the device off. The wheels and rods slowed. The device fell silent. Only the odor remained, dissipating rapidly through the open door.

"Oh dear," said a nearby voice. Ms. Rawlings stood at the door.

"Hey this isn't—"

The small woman raised a silencing hand, shuffled slowly into the room. Elanor watched her, stunned. Ms. Rawlings paused at the table and pointed to Smith.

"We were hoping to steal this one's mind, the invading one, before it returned to the past. Long story. We call them 'Yithians', psychic explorers that exchange minds with the people of our time."

That nighttime vision, she thought. *The bronze egg.*

"Good. The transfer machine is still here and intact," Ms. Rawlings continued. "What about the stiff on the floor? Who is he?"

"My husband," Elanor replied. "Is his mind gone too? The cap wasn't on his head though. I just thought I'd electrocuted the bastard."

Ms. Rawlings leaned forward and scrutinized the device. "Worse than that dear. His mind is somewhere without a body. Wherever it is, I doubt his sanity is intact."

"It couldn't have happened to a better man," Elanor said with satisfaction.

"I saw him snooping around earlier. Is his body of any use to you?" Ms. Rawlings asked matter-of-factly. Examining a concave mirror, she turned it slightly.

"Er no. Not at all. Good riddance."

"Marvelous," Ms. Rawlings replied. "One of my friends can dispose of these human shells." The little woman licked her pale lips. The tongue was black and slimy.

"You're not quite human yourself, are you," Elanor said, as a statement more than a question.

Ms. Rawlings tapped her nose and smiled wryly. "I will keep your secrets if you keep mine."

Mr. Smith twitched. Elanor nearly jumped out of her skin.

Ms. Rawlings laughed. "Oh. He survived the transition. This is the body's original owner by the way. Will he have some stories to tell."

She clasped her hands together. "Callooh Callay! Such a productive day. Now be a dear and leave me alone here. You may even want to vacate the house for a little while."

Elanor didn't need telling twice.

The Beldam of Bedlam

by Ash Hartwell

The ornate gardens were spacious and colourful, a place of peace and tranquillity sitting in stark contrast to the chaotic cacophony awaiting beyond the hospital's iron-bound oak doors. Lawns smooth enough to play croquet on and manicured hedges lined the approach to a decorative fountain, which trickled water into a small reflecting pool, although I doubt many of the residents had ventured forth to reflect on the circumstances of their incarceration.

I alighted from my carriage, instructed the driver to get himself some refreshment from the kitchen, and banged on the door with the pommel of my walking cane. There was the sound of heavy bolts being drawn and the rattle of a key turning in a lock before the door swung open. The wood juddered and creaked as the door scraped across the stone floor. The darkness beyond reached out as if eager to enfold me in the malevolence lurking beyond the threshold. At my back was warmth and sunlight, birdsong, and the sweet scent of spring. Before me, a void, divest of warmth, from which seeped the foetid stench of malaise.

I stepped inside, and a disembodied voice, my eyes not yet having grown accustomed to the dark, greeted me.

"Good afternoon, sir."

A ghost-like image drifted in the shadows behind the door. Pale and translucent, it lacked shape or substance. I blinked away the sunlight's dancing phantoms as the door creaked closed behind me. Before me, the ghost took shape. A starched white pinafore covered a dark dress, and a stiff cap enclosed a mass of hair pinned up in a severe bun. The face was fresh and feminine, yet austere.

"And a good afternoon to you, miss." I pondered whether to give her my hat and cane, unsure of the etiquette.

"Doctor Bartholomew is expecting you, sir." Her hands remained clasped together, solving my conundrum. I shall keep my hat and cane, at least for the time being.

"Thank you. Although I am a little early, I'm afraid."

"Punctuality is a virtue, tardiness a vice, as my mother used to say, sir."

"An astute observation, and one I shall endeavour to remember."

A flicker of a smile touched the young woman's lips, yet she appeared ill at ease. Perhaps she was unused to such social intimacy with Doctor Bartholomew's learned visitors.

"Please forgive me if I have spoken out of turn. It was not my intention to cause you discomfort," I said, offering her a slight bow and noticing she had a bandage on her hand, an occupational hazard I assumed in this place.

"There is nothing to forgive, sir. Your generosity towards my mother's proverb overwhelmed me for a moment, nothing more." She tried to hide her bandaged hand behind her skirts, so I decided not to mention it to avoid further embarrassment on both our parts.

It was I who now felt ill at ease. I mumbled an awkward and dismissive acknowledgement as I removed my gloves.

Recovering her previous austere demeanour, the young woman hurried away, her full skirts rustling and rippling in her wake. "Doctor Bartholomew has not yet finished his rounds. If you will be so good as to follow me, I shall show you to his study."

I had to hasten my stride to keep pace with her as she led me along a wide corridor with a black and white chequered floor and a potent scent of carbolic. At the head of a wide flight of stairs, she opened a door and stepped aside to allow me entry to the room beyond.

"Please make yourself comfortable, sir. The doctor will not be much longer." The young woman hesitated for a moment as if to say something further, but then thinking better of it, pulled the door closed.

Doctor Bartholomew's study had a suffocating and oppressive atmosphere. Dark wooden floorboards covered in part by a Chinese styled rug and heavy full-length curtains set the tone, while bookcases overflowing with thick leather-bound tomes lined one wall. The far wall was dominated by a tall window, in front of which sat Doctor Bartholomew's cluttered desk. Two high-backed chairs and a small circular table set with decanters and glasses occupied the centre of the room. The only light came from the window, but as this looked out onto a small interior courtyard, it only further added to the room's unwelcoming ambience.

I considered pouring myself a drink but decided that would be a gross imposition on Doctor Bartholomew's hospitality, so I amused myself by perusing his comprehensive library of medical and scientific volumes. My inspection had not gone further than the first shelf when the door opened, and the diminutive statue of Doctor Bartholomew swirled into the room. What the doctor lacked in height, he made up for in girth and in the gregarious nature of his character. Intelligent, witty, and outspoken to a fault, I had witnessed the doctor dominate even the most learned of gatherings.

"I am so sorry to have kept you waiting, Your Grace." He crossed the room, arm extended. His handshake was firm and vigorous.

"Please, call me Edward. I have not yet grown accustomed to my new titles, and I am too young for such stuffy formality."

"Queen Victoria is but a slip of a girl herself. Perhaps your inexperience of stuffy formality goes in your favour."

"Perhaps so. But I would like to think my appointment came about because of my scientific knowledge. It is my intention to use modern scientific methods, not religious zeal, to investigate allegations of witchcraft and draw logical conclusions. The Queen wishes to remove the crime of witchcraft from the statute books so it can not be used to persecute women."

"Indeed. A noble cause, although one that will meet much resistance from the Church. But enough politics. And you are well?" the doctor asked as I slid a book back into its place on the bookcase.

"Is business so slow you need to drum up trade?" I asked with a smile.

"There is no need. Madness lurks in every corner of London."

"Or sits in the Palace of Westminster."

Doctor Bartholomew's deep chuckle filled the room. "Those are your words, not mine."

"Spoken like a true politician," I replied, joining in with his laughter.

"Come, let me show you the sights of Bedlam, one of London's leading attractions. You wish to meet with the beldam, but a little context does nobody any harm." Doctor Bartholomew escorted me from the room like an excited puppy.

We passed through several locked doors, Doctor Bartholomew opening each one with a key hanging from a large ring on his belt. With each door we passed through, the sounds and smells of Bedlam intensified. Wild screams rent the air, cackles of laughter filled the corridors, and the stench of human waste and unwashed bodies cloyed at the throat.

"Do you ever get used to the smell?" I asked, pressing a handkerchief to my mouth and nose.

"Not entirely. But lavender essence helps." Doctor Bartholomew handed me a tincture in a small bottle. "Place a few drops on your handkerchief."

I did as he instructed. The sweetness of the lavender disguised the odour but did not eliminate it. I could understand why ladies and gentlemen of a delicate disposition swooned during their visit to Bethlem Royal Hospital. I could afford no such luxury as I had a duty to perform. Doctor Bartholomew led me deeper into the maelstrom of madness, and I tried to close my senses to the surrounding depravity.

All those we encountered had shaven heads, some with open wounds on their scalps. Men and women urinated and defecated in their rooms; I hesitate to call them cells, yet that is what they were. Some lay in soiled bedding. Others had no bedding or even a bed. A naked woman ran past us shrieking, a guard or perhaps another patient, in pursuit. There appeared little distinction or division between the sexes. Several of the younger women looked pregnant, and in one room a couple were fornicating before a cheering crowd of onlookers.

I witnessed people chained to the wall, a man having his head held under water as a priest prayed for his soul, and two men being forced to fight over a bowl of cold gruel while the guards placed bets on the winner. And all the while, the stench of rot and decay filled the damp air. Wounds festered with maggots. Scabies and lice infested skin, clothing, and bedding alike. In one dark cell, rats gnawed on an arm protruding from a bundle of dirty blankets and straw. Doctor Barthlomew took it all in stride, pointing out success stories and describing the latest treatments with pride, his eyes blinded to the depravity that existed all around.

At last, we arrived at a door at the end of a corridor. A guard stood outside with a cosh, or perhaps a cudgel would be a better description given its size, resting across thick forearms. A brazier, its flickering flame casting strange dancing shadows on the rough stone walls, burned in an alcove set in the opposite wall.

"Here we are. The famous Beldam of Bedlam. Witch, sorceress, murderess. Pick your poison, after all, she did." Doctor Bartholomew's complexion had grown sallow, his breathing laboured, perhaps down to the exertion of our journey, but I saw fear in his eyes.

"As there is no such thing as witchcraft or sorcery, I pick murderess. Potions are nothing but medicines, no different from those you prescribe, doctor. Spells and incantations are just prayers. Mere words uttered with devotion and belief. The woman behind this door is just that... a woman. A mad, deluded woman who experiences hallucinations and palsies, but no witch." I spoke with what I hoped sounded like authority and conviction, although I confess, I felt little of either.

The atmosphere in the narrow corridor hung heavy and damp; a coarse, dark blanket that smothered reason and hope. I tried to dismiss the feeling, telling myself it resulted from some shared psychosis, a communal sense of mistrust and fear which my senses, heightened by expectation, had dialled into. Like a child who cannot sleep after hearing a ghost story on All Hallows Eve, I did not believe, but I could not dismiss.

"Either way, Your Grace. I will go no farther. Johnston here," Doctor Bartholomew waved a dismissive hand towards the guard, "will accompany you inside."

Johnston gave a polite nod and took a single key from his pocket. I noticed a chain attached it to a loop on his belt. Doctor Bartholomew hurried away at a pace comical for a man of his stature. I watched him go. The haste and rudeness of his departure both perplexed and astounded me. How could a man of such eminence and learning be so afraid of something as absurd as witchcraft that he abandons his guest in such a manner?

I pondered this question for a moment and decided the answer, whether logical or fantastical, lay beyond the old woman's cell door. Whatever the truth, her deeds and the rumours that accompanied them stretched far beyond the institution's thick, stone walls. If that were not the case, I would not have made the journey here. In a bizarre twist, my presence gave credence to the very imputations I wished to dispel.

"Are you ready, sir?" Johnston's voice broke my reverie.

I nodded, unsure I could trust my voice not to betray me. The weight of expectation and the doctor's strange behaviour had combined to cause a fluttering in my chest and a stricture at the base of my throat. A lesser man would have called it fear, but I had nothing to fear.

Johnston turned the key, unlocking the door with a reassuring clunk. He pushed the door open with his cudgel, peering into the shadowy half-light beyond. A blast of air, so cold it turned my breath to vapour, pierced my clothing. I imagined my bones cracking, the image so vivid I felt compelled to shake my head.

"You will get used to the heat in a moment. It's always the same, even in mid-winter, as if the fires of Hell warmed it," Johnston said, sweat slicking his hair to his forehead.

I shivered, regretting my decision to divest myself of my cloak in Doctor Bartholomew's study. With hesitant steps, I edged into the beldam's lair. The shadows seemed to swirl and solidify around me, then, just as I thought somebody touched my arm, they evaporated.

I heard a sigh. So close, the warmth of somebody's breath tickled my ear. With a mixture of surprise and curiosity, I swung round just as Johnston stepped in behind me, brandishing a flaming torch.

Light chased the shadows away, and I found nobody stood beside me. I laughed, embarrassed at my reaction, then sucked in a deep draught of air which felt like a thousand needles pricking my lungs. The pit of my stomach roiled like a storm swept sea, my muscles felt tense and taut.

Johnston kicked the door closed behind us, but ventured no further. He held the cudgel aloft, his elbow bent. The crackling torchlight caught the whiteness of his knuckles, and the wildness of his eyes. I tried to relax, to ignore Johnston's superstitious ignorance, but the air held a charge, the sort that builds on a warm evening before a storm.

Giving Johnston what I hoped was a reassuring smile, I turned to survey the room. Larger than I expected, with four stone walls of equal length with no windows or any other features apart from the one door. A low wooden cot lay against the wall farthest from the door. A bundle of dirty straw and filthy and torn blankets served as bedding. No other furniture occupied the room. Of the woman I had come so far to visit, there appeared no sign.

Confused, I looked to Johnston for an explanation. Had they brought me to the wrong cell? Had I come too late and she had died, her body already removed? Her exact age remained unknown, although many believed her already a centurion. But if that was so, why had nobody told me? Why the farce of bringing me all the way down here?

Then the bundle of rags and straw moved. At first, it was nothing more than a gentle rustling of the straw, a disturbance in the folds and creases of the rags. Then a figure emerged, rising as though a waking giant might arise from beneath a hillside. An outstretched arm, reaching upwards. Head. Shoulders. The bundle of rags slipped away as more of the figure revealed itself. The giant's hillside crumbled into the valley below.

Feet, sinewy and calloused, nails curled like talons, dropped to the floor. A cough, thick and wet, wracked the air. The figure sat on the edge of the cot, head down. Drool hung in a glistening stalactite from beneath the mass of wiry white hair until a clawed and twisted hand wiped it away. A loose-fitting gown, once white but now grey and stained, hung off one emaciated shoulder. What skin was visible in the eerie yellowish lamplight appeared scabbed and dirty. An open wound on the knee oozed a festering mixture of blood and puss, providing a feeding and breeding ground for the cloud of flies, the drone of their wings giving the room a voice of its own.

Johnston remained behind me. The light from his lamp came over my left shoulder, my shadow a tall dark stain on the far wall. I shuffled forward, no longer so confident in my conviction that the Beldam of Bedlam was nothing more than a harmless old crone.

I had long suspected fear a contagious emotion, and as I stood there, in the beldam's evil presence, I knew myself infected. Fear had surrounded me the moment I entered the institution's impressive doorway. I had inhaled it. Absorbed it. Immersed myself in it. I realised in that moment the remedy to this malaise lay not in science and medicine, but in my heart.

Courage. The cure lay in courage. If I showed courage, it would spread. Like the infection, the remedy would transmit and transfuse itself, person to person. Doctor Bartholomew, Johnston, and the young woman who had welcomed me would regain their strength. The strength to overcome the fear paralysing their every thought, deed, and action.

Then the beldam spoke. Each dry syllable grated against the soft, pink flesh of my ear before echoing through my head, shredding my nerves. Nails dragged down a blackboard could not have set my teeth more on edge than this old woman's voice.

"So, you have come to visit the famous Bedlam Beldam." It was not a question, nor did it sound like a statement. It was a simple observation, as if she had expected my visit, yet my presence somehow disappointed her.

I summoned my courage, conscious my first words must convey the authority bestowed upon me. "If you believe yourself famous, madam, then you have misjudged the public mood. They loathe you. Detest you, even. Do not confuse fame with infamy."

The figure shrugged. "Fame. Infamy. Two sides of the same coin. The truth remains: when they write the history of this vile institution, I shall command a chapter while you will appear as a mere footnote in my story."

"I do not seek fame for myself. If I warrant a footnote, it will be as the man who dispelled the myth of the infamous Beldam of Bedlam as I did The Whitechapel Witch."

At the mention of Gwendoline Hooper's supernatural sobriquet, the beldam lifted her head, and I saw her worn and wrinkled face for the first time. A prominent forehead, dirty and scabbed, dropped to sunken eye sockets concealed beneath an overgrown hedgerow of eyebrow. A wide nose sat askew above thin, pale lips. Hair grew above the upper lip and sprouted from a wart just below the pudgy chin. Rough, heavy jowls hung from the face like empty sacking. Yet, for all the ugliness of age and a life lived in poverty, the eyes kept the lustre and brightness of youth. They reflected the spluttering torchlight like pools of liquid fire, threatening to engulf everything in their sight.

My breath caught in my throat and my guts turned to water. I have never experienced fear so real. So immediate. I was sure an inexperienced soldier awaiting the order to charge headlong into the enemy's cannons would not feel the same terror. He had comradeship and honour and at least some command of his destiny, while I perhaps just had honour, although at that moment I did not feel honourable. I may not have believed her a witch, but in that moment, I believed the Devil had command of her soul.

"Gwen Hooper was a crazy old woman. The simpletons who mistook gossip for gospel gave her mythological status. In truth, the ugly old crone didn't even live in Whitechapel." The beldam cackled to herself, but the expression in her eyes remained unchanged.

"And I proved the myth a lie..."

"And left her hanging from the gallows," the beldam shouted, interrupting me. Once the echo of her words had died away, she added, "So, what did you achieve?"

"I proved..."

"I proved," the beldam lampooned my voice, making me sound both baleful and childish.

I remained silent, letting my anger subside. In just a few minutes, this old crone had both shattered my confidence in the mission I had undertaken and undermined my achievements. My disbelief of the supernatural remained firm, yet this bent and frail old woman possessed an aura of evil, but it was an evil rooted in the sins of humanity.

The beldam rose on unsteady legs and stood just a few feet in front of me. Johnston lifted the lamp higher, and my shadow shrank in response. The old woman's thin smock was filthy, large dark stains marked both the crotch and armpits, and hung from her frail, shapeless body.

I had hitherto grown accustomed to the cell's stench, but now it washed over me in bitter, putrid waves. The fetor of her unwashed body, her shit and piss, and the warm decaying rot of her breath, all combined to claw at the lining of my throat. I gagged, choking on the thick bile that filled my throat and burnt the thin membranes at the top of my nose.

My eyes stung. I reached for my handkerchief, determined not to vomit. A hand gripped my elbow, and I realised Johnston was offering me support, both tactile and emotional. Holding my linen handkerchief to my nose, I squared my shoulders. Drawing myself up to my full height, I towered over the diminutive beldam.

Undaunted, she looked up at me, her gaze somewhat sideways, and I noticed she carried herself with a slight hunch. She looked amused, curious even, but her eyes held no fear as they darted across my face as if searching for something. A physical blemish perhaps, or a weakness in my character that my countenance betrayed.

"You're a strong young man, one of England's finest, I'll warrant. Good family, expensive education, membership of the right clubs, dining at the best restaurants. Titled nobility, a landed gentleman." Her lips twisted in a cruel sneer, each word carrying an accusation.

"And you are a mad old woman. Uneducated. Abandoned by her family and left to die in the bowels of Hell." My retort sounded peevish, almost childish.

"And yet, which of us is more frightened? I have nothing; therefore, nothing to lose. You, on the other hand, have everything to lose. Respect and standing, wealth and privilege, a life, a family. Even death holds no fear for me. You could take me to the gallows this very evening, but it will only set me free."

"Free from this place or your own madness?" I asked, aware Johnston was shuffling from foot to foot behind me, eager to escape this woman's domain.

"Persecution. You may not believe me a witch, but there're plenty who do. I can understand their persecution, it comes from fear on the stories they were told as children, on superstitions handed down through generations of God-fearing families, on the misguided words of papal bulls and royal decrees, but you persecute me for the simple fact I am a woman." She raised her voice in anger, grabbing at her breasts as if to highlight her sex.

I wiped her spittle from my face before replying. "I do not persecute women, or those given to madness, or even those who confess to fornicating with Satan. My mandate requires me to investigate the facts, to establish the truth, and to disprove the absurd."

"Then you watch them swing from the branch of the village's witching tree or the county gallows. Tell me, your lordship, how many women have you saved from having their necks stretched?" Sarcasm and scorn dripped from her every utterance.

"I do not save women from their crimes, only from the accusations of witchcraft or demonic collusion. Whether they hang for their crimes or die by their own hand in a fit of madness, it is of no consequence to me. Witchcraft is a superstitious belief held by zealots and used to control the ignorant."

"None, then." The beldam nodded to herself as if satisfied with her interpretation of my answer.

"It is for the courts to..." I tried to explain, becoming frustrated by her refusal to understand my position.

"Blah, blah, blah. Courts. Church. I'm not mad or fornicating with the Devil, but I am a witch. I do not confess it because to do so would suggest it is a crime or a sin that requires forgiveness, which it is not." She moved closer, challenging me to renounce her.

"Get back, Witch!" Johnston tries to step between us, his club raised.

Showing a fleetness of foot belying her age, the beldam lunged beneath his arm. I felt a searing pain on the back of my hand as I stumbled backwards in response to the melee in front of me.

The beldam cackled in excited laughter as Johnston hauled her off her feet and propelled her backwards, one arm around her wrinkled neck, the other twisting her wrist. I saw it fold double and heard the dry snap of bone.

My hand felt wet, sticky. I glanced at it and I was surprised to see two deep scratches running from my wrist to the base of my fingers. In the cell's darkness, my blood appeared black as I fumbled for a handkerchief.

Johnston forced her back towards her pile of rags. Her hand hung limp and useless from her wrist, but she continued to cackle, oblivious to the pain. The cackle had become less humorous and more demented, the sound echoing around the cell's bare walls.

As I watched, she lifted her useless hand to her mouth, my blood dripping from her gnarled fingers. Blood smeared her lips as she placed her fingers in her mouth, her tongue flicking back and forth as she licked them clean.

I hurried from the room as Johnston forced the old woman to the floor. It took him far longer to subdue her frail physique than it should have, and all the while, her laughter grew louder and more maniacal.

Johnston stumbled into the corridor as I knotted the handkerchief, forming a makeshift bandage. He swung the door shut with a loud clang, turning the key in the lock before allowing himself to sink to his knees.

"Are you alright, sir? I didn't know she would attack you. Honest, I didn't." Johnston sounded both apologetic and frightened. I wondered if the beldam's actions or the consequences he might incur for allowing a visiting dignitary to come to harm caused his fright.

"Yes, I'm fine. Thank you, Johnston. Without your quick actions, I could have suffered far worse injuries," I replied, offering him a brief and, what I hoped, reassuring smile.

"Your Grace?" The old woman said from her straw and rags. A door and several strides separated us, yet I heard her words as if she had whispered in my ear. I went to the door, but did not reply.

"I know you're there, Your Grace. Heed my words. I will be free of this accursed prison before you breathe fresh air again."

After those words, she fell silent. I waited for a few moments, unsure whether to reply, then, thinking better of it, followed Johnston back up through the maze of corridors.

"I will instruct Marie to find a suitable bandage for your hand," Johnston said, delivering me to Dr. Bartholomew's study. "Good day, Sir."

"Good day to you, sir." I watched Johnston leave, his rough-and-ready presence incongruous with this part of the building, before I knocked.

Receiving no answer after my second, and louder knock, I entered anyway, assuming the doctor would not mind me warming myself with his whiskey. I poured a drink and settled into a chair to ruminate on my meeting with the fabled Beldam of Bedlam and awaited my host.

A knock disturbed my reverie, and I bade the visitor, "Enter."

The young woman I had met earlier entered, a tray in her hand. "Mr. Johnston said the beldam injured your hand."

"Marie? Yes, but it is a trivial scratch."

"Nothing the beldam does is trivial. She wanted your blood. It's the source of her magic." Marie set the tray down and showed me her bandaged hand.

"The beldam?"

Marie nodded.

"There is nothing to fear. She is no more a witch than I am a horse."

Marie laughed, but she still looked troubled as she dressed my hand. Her touch felt gentle, and she had a habit of poking her tongue out of the side of her mouth when concentrating. Her beauty, which I had not noted on my arrival, took my breath away. We made polite small talk as she worked, and I became captivated by her charm.

"A messenger came calling Dr. Bartholomew away, and we are not expecting him back until late. Perhaps I could walk you to your carriage?" Marie's gaze held mine, and despite the impropriety of her suggestion, I could not, nor did I want to, refuse.

Marie escorted me back through the reception area to the main entrance and out to my waiting carriage. It seemed natural she should take my arm as we walked, even climb into the carriage with me.

As the carriage bore us through the gardens and back onto the principal thoroughfare, we settled into the comfortable silence of two people at ease with each other.

"Will your presence not be missed?" I asked after a few minutes as the hospital receded into the distance.

"No more than yours," cackled the Beldam of Bedlam as she lunged across the carriage, her keen, emaciated fingers tearing at my throat.

Blanky

By Thomas Folske

In the beginning, it did not feel. At least, it knew not of any feelings it may have ever had. It was simple, a piece of fabric cut and manufactured to the retailer's specifications. Its design, an assemblage of owls and Christmas elves against a red background, was one of many that the factory produced. It was nothing exceptional. It was just like all the rest of its genderless, thoughtless, lifeless, identical siblings. It knew nothing. It wanted nothing. It was simply content and did not even know that it was content. It did not think, but if it had thoughts they would have been complacent thoughts. It was made to be a slave, an object, created by makers as unaware of its potential self-awareness as it was. It was a blanket, nothing more, nothing less, just like all the other blankets around it.

That was and had always been the only existence it knew, though it did not know, for it did not think. It was an inanimate object. Just a child's blanket, no different from the millions of others of its kind all around the world. The factory world was meaningless. So was its loading onto a truck and being shipped to a retail store. At that point, even if it had ripped or been destroyed it would not have cared. It could not care.

Upon arriving at its destination, the blanket was unloaded and eventually placed upon a shelf, to which it was completely indifferent. There it remained for many days and nights, being walked past by scores of people and inspected by a few. Some of its siblings had even been purchased, never to be seen again, but it didn't notice or care. It didn't care about anything. It had no affinity for the blankets that looked just like it, nor toward any other blankets, nor toward anything at all for that matter. It just was, and life went on around it, and even if it hadn't, the blanket would not have cared either way.

Until one day, while the blanket was doing nothing other than being a blanket, a woman with streaks of gray in her hair walked up to the piece of fabric, looked at it, picked it up, then put it in her cart without another thought. The blanket also accepted this act without even a first thought.

It went for a car ride. Nothing. It got brought into a house and set in a closet. Still nothing. It sat in that closet for close to two months, the majority of the time in complete darkness, and still it felt nothing. It didn't care when it was finally taken out of the closet, nor when it was enclosed in a colorful paper cocoon and placed beneath a tree it could not see. It showed no emotion at all when a little boy finally ripped the paper enclosure apart, tugged the blanket out of its wrappings, and threw it on the floor, only to make way for another treasure hidden by a thin barrier of festive decorations.

The blanket spent some time on the floor before, at some point, being accidently kicked under a chair. There it stayed until the house had become quite dark. That was when a different woman than the purchaser, a woman without gray streaks in her hair, found it, pulled it out of its ersatz cave, and carried it across the house to a sofa that was equally as content as itself. The blanket was too busy not caring to care, when all of a sudden it was draped across something small and warm that wriggled lightly beneath its weight, clutching part of its fabric body tightly in his small arms. It was the first truly loving embrace the blanket had ever experienced. It was at that moment, that very instant, the blanket did something it had never done before. It did something it didn't even know it could do. Even though it was only the slightest shadow of an inkling of a feeling, the blanket felt.

It didn't realize what was happening at first, and although it knew it shouldn't care, humored the experience. Whatever was happening wasn't like being ripped or even burned, neither of which would have bothered it. No, this was something internal. It was an indescribable sensation running through every fiber of its fabric. A sensation it didn't know how to deal with, being as it wasn't just the pure, undiluted contentment it had always known.

Ultimately, the blanket couldn't have done anything even if it had wanted to, so it didn't. It just focused on being held. It focused on the love and need resonating off the child it was covering, and to say it enjoyed that experience would be an overstatement. Its inklings were far from that well refined but were at least echoes of joy, and on this first night that was truly all the blanket could handle.

The blanket did not have any need for sleep nor food, nor did it have any concept of time, energy, or any other things that living beings needed to worry about. Everything that the blanket was and knew was generated from the boy who now lay beneath it.

For most of the next day the blanket sat motionless and thoughtless, but that night, when the boy got tired, he went and looked for the blanket. The two spent another night together, and the love the blanket felt made it just a little more aware of itself.

This went on for weeks, causing the blanket, who affectionately began to be known as "Blanky", to gradually feel and comprehend more and more love and affection. The boy, who Blanky had heard, or at least registered, was called Franklin Halverson, who continued to want and need it each night.

Franklin loved Blanky, and although Blanky did not know or understand it, and wasn't quite at the capacity to do so, it was beginning to love Franklin as well. Even though Franklin drooled on Blanky practically every night and peed on it about once every other week. It felt the boy's pee, but that was just a meaningless physical sensation, like the drool, or being left on the floor and stepped on, or dragged across mud and washed and dried countless times. None of that mattered, or even compared to what Blanky felt when Franklin held it close and nuzzled his loving face into its softness.

If Blanky could have moved it would have shown Franklin that it loved him back, but it couldn't move, could barely feel, and inherently knew it wasn't even supposed to be able to do that.

For every wave of love Franklin sent Blanky, Blanky stored as much of each as it could, trying to process and understand what it was now having to, and also wanting to endure. As Blanky gradually started to become self-aware, it also seemed to choose to ignore the parts of its existence that didn't involve the boy, much as it did with Franklin's pee.

All Blanky cared about was Franklin and the love, an energy immeasurable by human standards, that Franklin freely passed onto it.

Months went by and Blanky, having survived every accident, over-strenuousness, and blatant but unintentional inconsideration, still felt for (loved) Franklin just as much, and truthfully more, than the first day he had been draped over the diminutive sleeping child. Blanky didn't feel things physically, it knew it was spilled on and stepped on and stuff, but it also, technically, didn't actually feel the hugs from Franklin. It was the small boy's love that made the hugs real, the emotion made it so Blanky could feel them.

Blanky wasn't the only one to feel the love grow, but unlike Blanky, who had to gradually start to feel anything at all, Franklin's mind was an explosion of intense feelings. His love for Blanky had been practically immediate, and after only a few days it was stronger than Roman concrete and deeper than The Mariana Trench... and growing. In fact, Franklin would cry, scream, and freak out if he forgot Blanky. Both his mother and father caved every time and turned back to get it, no matter how far away from home they had come.

Franklin felt protected by Blanky, and Blanky felt protective of Franklin. Though aside from providing him warmth in the night or during a nap in the car, Blanky couldn't provide an actual deterrent against anything truly harmful. His material was soft, thin. It couldn't even provide the simple protection of leather, and if it rained Blanky couldn't keep Franklin dry. As for the ability to stop a physical force trying to do him harm, Blanky was incapable of doing anything at all. Still, Blanky felt protective, and if he could be or do anything to protect Franklin in any situation, Blanky would sacrifice itself a thousand times over.

Thankfully, Franklin's parents protected him from rain by bundling him in the correct attire and preventing him from going out in too harsh conditions, and they protected him from doing dangerous things via reprimands, and they even protected him from bad environments and dangerous people by avoiding questionable places and monitoring where and with whom Franklin went.

They all had a good thing going, Blanky, Franklin, and Franklin's parents... that is until they moved to the new house about eight months after Blanky had first been introduced into Franklin's life.

From the moment Franklin first crossed the threshold of the new place, cuddling the majority of Blanky while dragging a small portion of it on the floor, Blanky felt something it had never felt before. Something of similar power to Franklin's love, but in the complete opposite direction. Just like love, Blanky did not know what this new feeling was at first, but in its very essence it knew the sensation was not good. Blanky would have not liked it, not at all, had it had any preferences in such matters, but it really only cared about its love for and from Franklin. Also, if Blanky had understood feelings better and knew their names, it would have known at that moment it'd had its first experience with both fear and dread.

The negative feelings were always present in the house, but for the most part they were overshadowed by Franklin's love. Except in his bedroom. Blanky could always feel those malignant expressions of evil the strongest there, worse than absolutely anywhere else in the entire house, especially at night. It was in that room that Franklin woke up from every single nap crying, but not when he fell asleep in any other room in the house. It was there he had nightmares every single night, to the point that his parents fully expected they would be sharing their bed with their son before morning.

At first, Franklin's mother and father assumed it was the move that had caused Franklin's loathing of being in his room. But after almost two months of non-stop night terrors, in which Blanky could feel Franklin's panic, his fear, his distress, as well as the vile, repugnant feeling emanating from Franklin's closet, his parents began to grow concerned. They were curious about other possible causes for Franklin's issues, wondering if perhaps something mentally or emotionally triggering was happening. Franklin was only four and wouldn't go to school until next year. His only babysitter was his maternal aunt. They hoped it wasn't a developmental or cognitive problem, but they couldn't be sure. Ultimately, they just wanted to figure out what was wrong with their child.

Hesitant to initiate the act of taking Franklin in to get tested, his parents began grasping at straws and trying different things. One night, they had Franklin sleep on the couch, and, alas, he slept comfortably the whole night through. They tried a similar experiment in the spare bedroom, and even on an air mattress on the living room floor, and in every instance, Franklin slept fine. If he did wake up or stir, it was only to use the bathroom or something of the like.

Franklin's parents were confused. That was when Franklin's father, Jeff Halverson, had the idea to set up a camera in Franklin's room to see how, and possibly even why, Franklin was waking up each night.

The first night, they caught video of Franklin shortly after three in the morning, bolting straight up in bed as if a firecracker had gone off under his pillow. He immediately started to scream and cry, then ran through the open bedroom door and out into the hallway. His mother and father let him and Blanky come lay down in their bed and fall asleep again as his father watched the video of his son's terrifying emergence from sleep, focusing so hard on Franklin and everything around him that he missed the most important detail of all. Just a moment or two before Franklin bolted upright, screaming deliriously into the night, the door handle to his closet seemed to turn and open of its own volition, just a crack, but enough to let some of the darkness that was inside it come creeping out.

After scrutinizing the video for nearly half an hour, Franklin's father gave up on that particular occurrence and thus allowed another thought to enter his head. He scooped Franklin up out of their bed and returned him to his own room, never noticing in the process that the closet door remained ajar and had, in fact, opened just a little more while they had been away.

Franklin's father laid his son down in bed and Franklin immediately began to whimper and squeeze Blanky tightly, sensing something was amiss even as he slept, but he never woke up. Then Jeff Halverson did something he had never done before, he closed his son's bedroom door as he returned to bed.

After Franklin's father left, Blanky felt the malignance, the malevolence, the blasphemy of what was behind Franklin's closet door more powerfully than it had ever experienced anything, except for the first time it had been draped over Franklin, the first time it had been shown love.

Blanky didn't know what it was doing, didn't know if it could even do anything at all, but it knew it had to protect Franklin. It knew it had to do something, or at least try. What Blanky did then would be the equivalent of you or I trying to fly with imaginary wings or trying to use telepathy simply by concentrating and thinking of different things in different ways without any idea of whether or not we were even in the right ballpark for success. Blanky, on the other hand, as improbable as it may seem, was successful. Just slightly, it was able to shift itself about half an inch or so, not enough for Franklin's dad, who was watching, to have noticed, but enough for Blanky to have noticed. Even though it had no idea what it did to achieve such a feat, that didn't stop Blanky from trying again. It didn't know why, but the need for it to move seemed imperative to protect Franklin, and that maybe, if it didn't there might no longer be a Franklin to protect.

Blanky didn't understand life, let alone death, but it was starting to understand permanence and existence. It knew the meshing of the love that it associated with Franklin and the hatred that emanated from the closet would not be good, could not be good, as Blanky had a vague impression of just how delicate Franklin actually was.

While Blanky was trying to force itself into life, Franklin's father continued to watch the video record in real time, growing ever drowsier as he did so. Even though the likelihood of him noticing Blanky's nigh imperceptible movements were almost nil. Even if he had been wide awake and all the lights had been on, and it hadn't been the middle of the night, and he hadn't already been tired from the stress of Franklin's unidentified malady. Even if he wasn't exhausted from getting mostly broken or restless sleep, Jeff Halverson should have noticed the closet door creeping ever so slowly open. He should have noticed the shadow, darker than all the other shadows around it, slink stealthily, clandestinely, maliciously out of his son's closet and into his bedroom.

Franklin's father's eyes began to flutter, his whole body started to feel heavy, and to him, it looked like nothing at all suspicious was going on in his son's bedroom. He fell asleep staring at the screen that showed the nighttime room.

Blanky could feel the presence moving because it could feel the emotion of evil intent getting closer, stronger. It tried to move again, as it had done before, and to its utter joy not only moved of its own accord, but also moved further this time, faster and more forcefully.

Even if Franklin's father had stayed awake, as he would later find out when he reviewed the video, he wouldn't have seen what Franklin eventually saw, or what Blanky felt. No, he would have just watched portions of the room grow inexplicably darker as they began to form into vague shapes that were almost indistinguishable in the darkness. He wouldn't have seen what looked like long, insectile limbs with highly elongated fore and upper arms, thick, knobby elbows, and bony hands with thin, elongated fingers extending from the depths of the swelling shadow. He wouldn't have seen the thing attached to the shoulders of those arms dredge itself up slowly from the world of shadow and darkness, ever so gradually defining itself more and more, becoming increasingly tangible, increasingly corporeal, increasingly dangerous.

As the noxious creature emerged from the unfathomable depths of darkness below, Franklin began to sweat, to whimper, to cry. He squeezed Blanky tightly, feeling the fear caused by the monster's foul essence as it exuded into the air its unnatural presence and pheromones.

In his sleep, Franklin kicked Blanky off the lower portion of his body as he became drenched in sweat. The shadow creature's gently caressing, probing fingers reached the bottom of the bed, less than a foot away from Franklin's now exposed toes and feet. The poor young boy let out a small, desperate whine and he wet the bed.

Franklin felt the warmth and bolted upright in a panic, coming fully awake as he was still peeing. He instinctively went to hop out of bed and run to the bathroom when he saw it. The thing was beyond terrifying, a gaunt monster that looked like a rabbit forcibly combined with a gangly giant and a werewolf. It had a fuzzy, repulsive body that reminded Franklin of a spider, even though its shape was roughly that of a man.

Franklin screamed and grabbed Blanky tight. One of the creature's too-long arms reached toward him with fingers that were like snakes and curled them around one of his ankles, right before ripping him out of bed. The monster dragged him back toward the closet fast. So fast that, even though both Franklin's father and mother woke at the scream, and even though his mother came running instantly, Franklin would have been gone forever. He would have been taken into the world of shadows, stolen away, never to be seen again, before she even made it to the door. Franklin would have suffered the horrifying fate of possibly becoming food for the abomination that had snatched him, food for its abhorrent family or, worse yet, he might have survived in the darkness long enough to become one of the monsters himself.

As Jeff Halverson was awakened by his son's scream, his eye was attracted to movement on the screen viewing Franklin's bedroom. The room was dark, too dark to tell for certain, but it appeared as though his son was being dragged across the floor. Worse yet, there were four serpentine shadows prominently displayed on one of his legs, the one elevated and appearing as though it was being pulled. If Jeff hadn't known better, he would have thought those shadows looked a little like fingers, though not the digits of anything he had ever seen or heard of before.

He watched Franklin being pulled toward the abysmal darkness of the closet by the corporeal shadow. As his son was crossing the halfway point of his room, Jeffrey Allen Halverson witnessed something he never shared with another living soul, other than his wife, and they only talked about it once, for as long as he lived.

Franklin screamed in primal terror as the nightmare monster beyond anything he had ever dreamt of before pulled him toward the pitch-black void that was his closet. He knew his parents would never make it in time, so he clutched his blanket tightly in utter despair and surrender. Then, suddenly, Blanky jerked violently away from him.

Franklin and Jeffrey Halverson watched via different means, but with the same amazement as Franklin's blanket leapt out of the toddler's grasp and flew through the air at the shadow monster's throat. They both watched as the red Christmas blanket with elves and owls wrapped itself around the monster's neck like a mildly flamboyant boa constrictor, and it was at that point Jeff tore his gaze away from the monitor and ran full speed for his son's bedroom.

Blanky felt the evil presence from the closet grab onto Franklin's ankle. It felt them torn from the bed and yanked onto the floor. It felt the horror and abject terror as it pervaded and consumed all of Franklin's other emotions. All of Franklin's love was shadowed over with incoherent fear and Blanky couldn't stand it for one more instant. Blanky didn't care about itself or what it could or couldn't do. It just did. It did hard, and the next thing it knew, to its greatest delight, it flew full speed through the air, directly at the malignant thing that still had hold of Franklin.

Mary, followed by Jeff, burst into their son's room a moment later after having had to fight with the door handle. They saw Franklin lying on the floor crying, the shadow monster having apparently released him, but the boy seemed transfixed. He was staring up at the aberration that now tangoed with his blanket, his best friend, and couldn't look away. Jeff remembered what he had seen. As Mary ran to Franklin and fetched him up into her arms, Jeff ran toward the nightmare scuffle, joining the dark battle he understood nothing of by taking hold of the blanket before the shadow could reach the closet, knowing in his soul that this blanket had saved his son's life, no matter how absurd that seemed, and knowing that he owed it his own life for what it had done.

"Hit the lights, Mary! Hit the fucking lights!" Jeff screamed desperately.

Mary ran out of the room with Franklin in her arms as Jeff felt cold, infinitely black tendrils wrap around his flesh. He then relearned terror he hadn't known since he himself was a toddler. In the grip of this creature beyond any nightmare he'd had in decades, Jeff wet himself as the monster pulled both him and the blanket into the closet with it.

Mary burst back into the room a moment later, no longer burdened with the weight of their son, and flipped the light switch on.

At what seemed like the very last moment, Jeff jerked his son's blanket as hard as he could with both hands, tugging it away from the darkness and back into the light as the thing that Jeff could only register as the Boogeyman disappeared back into the incomprehensible blackness that lay beyond. Jeff and Blanky went flying backwards, Jeff landing on his back with the blanket on top of him as all the darkness in the room was consumed back into the closet, the door slamming shut in its wake with a bang that sounded like a shotgun blast.

Jeff got to his feet, running, fleeing from the closet door and holding his son's blanket as his wife stood at the threshold of Franklin's bedroom, urging him on. Once Jeff was outside the room, Mary slammed the door behind him, and together, Jeff grabbing Franklin who was standing in the hall just outside his bedroom, they fled the house and piled into the car. They ended up sleeping in a Target parking lot that night, but that was okay. There were no closets.

They put the house up for sale the next day, openly disclosing that it was haunted, and asking less even than what they had originally paid for it. It sold to a couple a few weeks later and they stayed at Mary's sister's place for the duration.

Jeff made sure Franklin always had his blanket with him, and they only went back to pack their stuff during bright daylight hours. On their first trip back, Jeff reviewed the tape, hoping to have caught on camera all that had transpired. To his chagrin, however, everything after the closet door had creaked open was full of static and was unwatchable. Jeff figured things as foul and unholy as he had seen that night probably weren't meant to be known anyway. Besides, there was always a chance that exposure to something like that might only make it stronger rather than give people the drive to kill it. Jeff fully believed people would much rather ignore a miracle, benevolent or malevolent, than consider it.

He kept the tape anyway, and even showed it to the guy who bought the house. The man was an amateur ghost hunter with his own internet show. He filmed an episode in the house which never aired, and that neither Jeff nor Mary ever saw, and four months later he killed himself.

Jeff and Mary made sure Blanky stayed with Franklin for as long as the boy would have it, and when he started to outgrow the blanket, they stored it in a box. Just over twenty years later, they gave Blanky to Franklin's two-year-old daughter, Melody. She squeezed the blanket tightly and smiled, loving it at first sight. It was the first time in over two decades that Blanky had been held. It instantly felt love again, and like no time at all had passed, it felt happiness. It vowed to love and watch over this little girl as it had watched over Franklin before her. Melody nuzzled her face into its soft fabric and fell asleep. Blanky gave her the most imperceptible hug.

Cruising With Honey Down Diablo Road

By J. Rocky Colavito

My mother abandoned us when I was three, so it's just been my dad, my dad's friends, their cars, and me. What little I remember of my mother is dark hair and eyes, a throaty laugh, a swaying, beckoning finger when she wanted me to come to her, collections of magazines about movies, and screaming, one-sided arguments demanding a different life in a warmer climate with my father.

She just up and left when my father had taken me out for ice cream. We returned home to an empty closet, a drained bank account, and a note I never saw. My father failed at holding back tears as he read it, grabbed his lighter, lit it, and threw it in the fireplace where we'd hung Christmas stockings on the mantle.

"It's just us, son." And he hugged me.

So, he and his group of friends who had a car club raised me and taught me about cars, alcohol (never that twain should meet), cigarettes, and women. Oh yeah, I learned all about women. How they looked, how they smelled, how they sounded when you treated them just right, what they hid, how they used you. An endless litany of the bad side of women led by my father and echoed by his friends. Truth be told, they were more in love with their cars, and I wondered, even at a young age, if maybe the effort that they put into their cars might have made a difference in their marriages.

But those were the cards I was dealt and it wasn't a horrible life. I learned how to fix just about anything that one can drive, had a never-ending supply of cars and parts to experiment on since my dad and one of his friends partnered up and bought a failing "You Pull It" junkyard and turned it into a thriving business. I worked there after school, on weekends, and during the summer, so I never really wanted for money or transportation. I had plenty of friends because I could always be counted on for a car or a tune-up. I didn't see the need for college, because I had a trade well before graduation. Dad and I were more like brothers than father and son, and his friends were a ready set of uncles who shared the same interests.

And, here and there, I'd hear from my absent mother. Never by phone or in person, but in the form of post cards from different places, a little souvenir, sometimes even a letter. Nothing beyond superficial; there would be the usual "I miss yous" or "wish you were heres" but nothing even remotely suggesting that she was sorry, or that she'd been wrong.

Despite all that happened, I didn't share their perspectives about women, and I did wonder from time to time why my mother up and left. More importantly, the little odds and ends showed that she was alive, and trying to stay connected, but left me wanting more.

I was seventeen when I got some puzzle pieces.

One of dad's friends had bought a new men's magazine. You know the kind, adventure stories, drink mixes, exotic locations, and pin-ups, lots of pin ups. Women in lingerie, women whose nudity was covered by a carefully placed potted plant, women with a shocked look on their faces as arms and hands covered their "accidental" exposure. It was called Double Dog Dare (the publisher obviously believed in truth in advertising), and the issue brought my father to his knees when he saw it.

He fell into heart wrenching sobs when he saw the centerfold. He screamed that it was his ex-wife, my mother. His friends tried to calm him as I scooped up the magazine for a look.

Her name is Honey Hoffman; 42-26-38. She's actually fully dressed, with her high heeled foot on the fender of the front end of a bright lime green T-Bird. Her skirt is slit along the side to expose a bright pink garter and the top of a black silk stocking. She looks out from the page, dark brown eyes boring into yours, a flood of brunette curls surrounding a fresh-looking face dotted with a few freckles, dominated by a suggestive smile. The caption reads, "Need a ride?" in harsh red lettering.

What tipped it was the hand with one beckoning finger raised. Damn me to hell, it was my mother when you put the parts together.

Dad spent the rest of that day drinking, his friends feeding him watered down scotch in the hope that he'd not notice. He went through the whole range of expected responses: embarrassment over her appearing in such a place, rage at having been abandoned, despondence over losing her. In spite of everything that we had to endure from being abandoned he still harbored some remnants of love for her somewhere in the bowels of his heart. He eventually passed out, a near empty bottle clutched in his hand. While they minded him, I took the magazine inside, figured out how to get hold of their office, and placed a phone call.

"Haygood Periodicals, how can I help you?" The feminine voice on the other end seemed a bit tired.

"It's about someone in one of your magazines."

"Which one?"

I gave her the name.

"I'll connect you, but I doubt you'll get very much."

"Thanks."

I was quickly connected, and just as quickly went on hold. I was on hold long enough to wonder about the growing phone bill when someone finally picked up. It was a guy this time.

"Who are you?" He was gruff.

I gave my name and stated my business.

"How do I know you're not a private detective, or a jilted lover?"

I politely answered that I believed that Honey Hoffman was my mother, and that I just wanted to see how she was doing.

"She abandoned you for a reason, kid. Let her alone."

I persisted, and at least managed to learn that she was alive, and seeming to be thriving. She was "going places" and currently moving from modeling to parts in movies.

"Matter of fact, kid, she's just wrapping something new right now, hot rod flick that the teens all cream over. It's called Cruising Diablo Road. She's the bad girl who comes to a bad end. Look for it in a couple of months." Then he hung up on me.

I resolved to keep an eye out for news of the film.

That news came two days later.

Honey Hoffman and her co-star Whip Wayland were both killed in an on-set accident. A stunt car went out of control and plowed into a crowd at the bottom of Diablo Road. The stuntman also died, and the car, a bright lime green T-bird (probably the one in the magazine) caught fire and exploded. Production was halted and the movie was scrapped. It made the national news, but my father was so inconsolable that it didn't register.

But it did with me.

I had plenty of money in the bank and a tricked-out Ford at my disposal. Since I hadn't taken a vacation in forever, my dad was willing to let me go. One of my "uncles" was at loose ends and he volunteered to come keep an eye on things.

I left on a Thursday in the morning, and struck out on Route 66, taking time to enjoy the sites. The sites were everything you'd expect, oddly themed hotels and restaurants, world's largest doohickeys, and lots of open spaces and weather that made me wish that the Ford was a convertible. The only weird thing I saw was lots of cars in that shade of lime green from the magazine. They'd either pass me going east, pull out of a way stop as I was pulling in, or lollygag ahead of me, prompting me to pass them. I made a mental note to find out the stock number on that color that I'd never seen before until that day with Dad.

I made it to Los Angeles one week later in the middle of the night, checked into one of those motels with a South Seas flavor, and slept until noon the next day.

The morning paper I had with my coffee informed me that I was just in time for Honey Hoffman's funeral. So, I scrambled to find some mourning clothes (paid a lot more than I should have, but it is LA after all), got directions to the cemetery, and arrived just in time for the graveside service.

There were only a few people there, four guys, four gals, one minister who looked like he really would rather have been elsewhere. The prayers were very non-specific; the service was quite perfunctory. I did manage to get to the side of the grave and drop a red rose onto the top of the coffin before the first spade of dirt fell. And that was that. No one queried my presence. And I just walked away, I figured I could visit the publisher tomorrow.

As I entered the parking lot by the cemetery I noticed a bright green T-bird at the outer edge, a high heeled woman in a tight white dress was putting on sunglasses and climbing into the car.

It pulled out, and slowly cruised toward me, I stepped back to let it pass.

It stopped next to me. The woman looked me up and down, dropped her sunglasses down her nose, cocked her head slightly and then said, "Need a ride?"

I took a step backwards. It was Honey Hoffman.

"Mom?" I stammered.

She laughed that laugh I remembered from childhood. "See you down Diablo Road, baby." She floored the T-Bird's accelerator and laid rubber out of the parking lot into slow moving traffic, blowing horns and screeching brakes soundtracking her exit.

I raced to my Ford, fumbled my way into it, and executed the same maneuver, barely missing a bread truck as I peeled out of the parking lot. I sped down two blocks, but the T-Bird was long gone.

I found a gas station. The pump jockey went about the ritual of filling the tank and washing the windshield. I stopped him at the oil and tire check.

"How do you get to Diablo Road?"

"Why do you want to go there? That place is cursed, more accidents there in a month than in a whole year in the rest of the valley. Some starlet just died there not two weeks ago."

I pressed and got what I needed. It was actually an hour's drive toward the ocean. I thanked him and set out. I had to know.

It was that time between late afternoon and dusk when I finally reached Diablo Road. It was clearly marked with signs signaling dangerous curves (quite ironic, I thought), warnings about using lower gears and no passing, and a handmade wooden sign indicating the number of deaths this year alone. The number 12 had been crossed out and the number 16's paint was still fresh looking. Knowing what I had to do, I geared up the Ford and started the drive.

Diablo Road was curvy, oftentimes giving little opportunity to maneuver. But I'm a great driver, and I had no fear of how this road shifted. I could barely make out a moving car ahead of me, throwing up dust as it gained speed to ascend. I coaxed more out of the Ford and got a little closer. I could see the bright lime green and the familiar back end of a T-Bird. It was the car.

I immediately sped up and closed the gap between us. Before long I was right behind it, inching closer. I don't know what made me do what I did next, but I pulled alongside it. The woman glanced over at me and threw me a smile. She accelerated.

So did I, and I flashed past her. I lost sight of her in my dust spew. Matter of fact, I lost sight of the road itself for a few moments because of all the dust. I felt a weird bouncing and grinding of gears that I've never known my Ford to do. I fought the wheel for a second, but finally brought the beast under control. I got cleared of the dust clouds and pulled off at the top of the mountain Diablo Road climbs. There's a scenic overlook there. After a minute, the T-Bird pulled up next to me.

Honey Hoffman exited, smiling, eyes welling, holding out her arms for a hug. We embrace, mother and son, finally. I started to stammer questions, but she put a finger to my lips.

"We'll have lots of time to catch up, sweetheart."

"What do you mean?"

"Baby, it's a long story."

"You said we've got time, why not follow me back to my hotel and . . ."

She threw back her head and laughed that unforgettable laugh. "Kinda hard to do that if you're dead."

"Huh?"

"Sweetheart, you wiped out just before you got up here. They'll find what's left of you and your car down in a ditch." She pointed down the mountain. I could barely make out an overturned car with flames licking around it.

"No way! Car's right here."

"Yes, and so's mine, I only got to go to my own funeral as a favor. Normally I can't leave here. I just spend the days and nights cruising Diablo Road." She took my hand and squeezed it. "At least now I'll have my grown-up son with me. Better than these old people and pimpled out teenagers."

She jerked her head to direct my gaze, I saw shimmering cars passing behind her, old and current, but all as shiny as they were when they rolled off the lots. Their drivers beeped and waved. My mother turned to blow kisses. She still held my hand.

As I yanked my hand away, I heard the familiar laughter once again and saw the T-bird, along with my mother, start to shimmer. I glanced down at my feet and saw the same shimmer. I felt less whole as I stepped back towards my Ford, which also seemed less solid. I suddenly didn't need to open the door to get in. The driver side window was down as my mother threw me a wink and gave me the come-hither finger.

"C'mon baby, we have eternity to cruise and get reacquainted." She powered up the T-Bird and took off in a cloud of dust.

I still had things I wanted to know, so I burned rubber after her.

If you hear of my death, try to break it to my father gently, or maybe don't, he might come out here himself, hoping we could be a family again.

But, as it stands, you'll find me and Honey Hoffman, my mother, on an endless cruise out here on Diablo Road. Heed the signs, because the number of deaths has been updated.

Need a ride? We're always looking for fellow cruisers.

Friend

Andy Holberry

"Give her back!"

Tommy lifted the doll higher than his sister could reach.

He was ten, she was six. He could outrun, outreach and out-think her. This was child's play. Literally.

"I think she needs a new head." He reached across with his other hand and grabbed the plastic doll's scrawny neck, and started to apply pressure.

"No... don't!" Maxi let out a scream that would have shattered glass had the range been slightly higher.

Tommy buried his head in one shoulder and covered his ear with the other hand. "Why, you little...!"

He pushed her in the chest and she sat down hard, the screaming stopped almost immediately. He smiled when he thought she was going to cry, but the expression fell from his face when he saw the look in her eyes.

"Shouldn't have done that. I'll tell on you." Her eyes were narrowed, her lips drawn down in a deep frown.

"Who? Who are you gonna tell? Mom is away, Dad's busy and won't believe you. So tell me," he sneered, with a very grown-up look on his young face, "who are you gonna tell?"

Maxi slowly turned her head and angled it towards the ceiling. Her eyes stopped on the small square there; the entrance to that darkest of places... the attic. She said something under her breath, just a single word so low it may have been a sigh. But he was sure he heard it.

"Friend."

Tommy followed her gaze and couldn't suppress the small shiver that rolled up his back. He didn't like it up there. He had been up once before with his father when the fuses had blown, plunging the space into complete darkness. The stacked boxes took on terrifying, just-seen shapes. The old coat rack was a monster with too many arms. The heap of old duvets and sheets was an amorphous blob coming to suck him into itself. The old decorations that peered out from damaged boxes were hands trying to drag him inside of their cardboard prisons.

When his dad had put a hand on his shoulder, he yelled as loud as he could. He dropped to the floor and curled into a tight ball until the lights returned. His mother downstairs threw the breakers. The electrics did that sometimes... it was an old house.

His dad had been on the other side of the room, eyes wide and staring at him. A part of him had wondered how his dad put an arm on his shoulder from way over there.

He looked at his sister again. She had been talking about this so-called 'friend' for a few days now. An imaginary friend? Someone to talk to? Maxi needed someone, he thought. She didn't have any real friends; Maxi was weird and would have had to make somebody up.

"Have your stupid doll!" With those words, Tommy yanked the head off the body and threw it out the open window. He dropped it on the floor and ran for the stairs. He knew she wouldn't tell their parents, she was too concerned about what would happen to the rest of her doll collection. There were so many heads just waiting to be plucked by a vengeful older brother.

Maxi gently picked up the doll, feeling wetness in her eyes as the tears threatened to run free. She stood and walked to the window, looking out. The grass outside was long, and had been for a while now. Dad had been meaning to mow it, but hadn't got around to doing so. Betty's head could be anywhere, and was probably lost forever.

She looked once more at the pale square that was the covered entrance to the attic and then at the space where her brother had been. Her eyes darted around, making sure she was completely alone.

"Ass!" She giggled.

Being just six, she didn't swear usually. She knew it was a 'bad' word, one that her mom and dad didn't want her to say. They would never hear her say it, not when they were around, anyway. But in private, alone, she was sure she could get away with it.

She heard whispering and concentrated. It may have just been the breeze moving the drapes at the window. May even have been the tallest of the branches on the nearby tree gently scratching on the glass. But she knew it wasn't. She cocked her head to the side, a smile playing at the corners of her lips as she listened.

"Oh, yes," she said in a low voice. "I'd like that."

Tommy opened the refrigerator and grabbed a juice box. He and Maxi had their favorites, and he picked up one of his. Thinking about it for a second, he grabbed the last of hers too.

Serves her right, he thought. Thinking she could scare me with an imaginary friend. He puffed out his cheeks, a small puff of air escaping his lips. He closed the fridge door and ran back to the stairs. As he passed the window, he looked outside. His dad was asleep in the deckchair. His shirt was off and he was soaking up the last of the summer sun. He wasn't a heavy sleeper, Tommy knew. If he or his sister needed anything, he would be there as quick as a flash.

At the top, he stopped, his head angled to the side in wonder. In front of him was one of his mother's large chocolate chip cookies. She shared them with the children, of course, but she always kept a few just for herself. And she only ever let them have one each. They were rich and moist, the huge chocolate chunks sitting in the dough like miniature islands. Tommy had peered closely at one before, had played scenes from his favorite sci-fi movie across the rugged cocoa landscape.

He leaned forward and picked up the cookie, bringing it slowly to his mouth. His teeth bit down, meeting the first piece of resistance. Then, he was through and into the softer, chewy center. As he chewed, he started towards his room only to see another cookie at the corner of the hall.

Okay, someone was playing a trick on him. He walked over to Maxi's door and pushed it open. His sister was lying on the bed, her head turned away from him. Her shoulders rose and fell gently, in sync with her breathing. He pulled the door closed behind him.

Tommy walked to the other cookie and picked it up too.

There was another further down the hall, and yet another near an open door.

Now, anyone older than him who had ever had this done to them before would realize something was wrong. But all he saw was food, delicious, scrumptious food. He wanted as many as he could get his hands on. He followed the trail of cookies to the door of the upstairs closet, and there he stopped.

On the one hand... it was a closet. He wondered what would happen if the door should close. He knew it would be dark in the small space, and also knew there was a cord he could pull which would activate the bulb hanging in the middle.

On the other... it was cookies. That oh-so delectable of foods. And there they were, staring back at him from the middle shelf. His mind told him he had had enough, that he didn't need the others. His stomach overrode and propelled his legs forward.

Tommy stopped at the threshold and reached forward, his fingertips almost touching the packet. He took a step closer... and was pulled inside by something he couldn't see. The door closed behind him, and he found himself in darkness.

Don't cry, he told himself. It's alright, just pull the cord. His hand waved around in the darkness until it found the dangling string. He gave it a pull. Nothing happened; the darkness remained.

Something moved in front of him. The cookies he was holding fell to the floor, and he stepped back as far as he could go. Something touched his face, and he let out a startled yell. It was cut short as something hard and small slammed into the space just below his ribs, stealing his breath. He gasped for air as the caressing touch came back. Something cold and metallic was pressed against his neck, and he had a fleeting moment to wonder what it was... Then he knew no more.

As Tommy fell, he had the impression of something small and fast climbing the shelves bolted to the walls. It, whatever 'it' was, would be headed for the panel in the ceiling. The panel that led into the attic.

As his blood plopped onto the floor, he could feel himself getting more and more tired. It was like going to sleep, apart from the sharp pain in his neck and the liquid clogging up his throat. As everything darkened, even more than what was around him, he heard a door open and then close downstairs.

His dad's voice, his 'annoyed because I was busy' tone, floated up to him through the locked door. "If you kids are messing around? I swear...!" Footsteps followed the voice. It was the last sound he heard.

Rita Barnes pulled her car into the drive at six minutes past five that same evening. The sun was just starting its slow descent. The shadows grew with each passing minute. She turned the key. The engine died off, the echoing growl of the V8 power-plant faded slowly in the still air.

Mark had not wanted her to drive the Dodge, but after her car broke, the engine mysteriously developing a rattle that no amount of investigation could find, he had to concede.

She looked out the open driver's window and saw the deck chair just peeking from the side of the house. That would be about right, she thought. While she was working, he would be out in the sun, ostensibly to mow the lawn and clean the gutters, but he wouldn't do either. Her husband of ten years would sit in the grass getting a tan. He wouldn't be asleep, just dozing, but he would put off the chores until he really had no choice but to complete them.

Opening the door, she stepped out into the still warm air that hadn't quite disappeared from the day. It had been a very good few days.

She looked up and could see nothing moving. Nobody ran out to greet her. She turned her head and took in the rest of the houses. Most of them were dark, with only a few showing lights here or there. They, as a family, kept to themselves. There was a 'vibe' here that didn't sit well with her, but the price they paid for the house was a steal.

Rita closed the door a little more forcefully than she should have and waited. If there was anything that would bring Mark running, it would be the thought of his precious car getting damaged.

She waited for a minute, then another. Five minutes passed before she realized... something wasn't right. She walked to the front door and pushed it open.

"Mark? Kids?" No answer. The air was still. The house had an empty feel to it.

"Guys, where are you?" She pushed the door closed behind her, put her bag down, and moved into the living room. Everything seemed to be where she had last seen it.

On closer inspection, the small table next to her husband's chair was tilted on its side. The same one he used to hold his drinks. It had fallen on its side, rucking up a corner of the rug in front of the fireplace. Not a big thing, not even much of a mess, but in a home that was always tidy it was something out of the ordinary.

Rita moved out of the room to the bottom of the stairs. She angled her head towards the back of the house, towards the kitchen, but could see no-one there. She peered into the shadows at the top of the stairs.

"Kids? It's mom. Come on now, stop playing around." Still, there was no answer. Motherly instinct took over, and she put a foot on the first step. The next was easier, and the one after that. The top of the stairs was almost in full dark, and she reached over to flick the light switch. Nothing.

She took a step, and her foot came down on something that crunched and shattered underneath her tread. She put a hand on the ground and lifted what was there towards her face. There was just enough light left to see the broken remains of the light bulb that had been removed from its housing.

Mark had taken the thing out? It could only have been him. The kids couldn't reach. But why? What was the reasoning behind it?

It was as she took another step, still deep in thought, that something else grabbed her attention. She could see. Not as well as if all the lights were on, but there was a thin sliver coming from down the hall. The soft glow lighting the edges of the wall, something was down at the far end of the house.

Around the corner, she followed the glow. It led her to one of the upstairs closets. In front of the door lay the remains of several cookies. Absently, she recognised the ones she had kept just for her, and as treats for the children.

Slowly, she reached out and grabbed hold of the slightly opened door and pulled it open. Her hand flew to her mouth. The scream that threatened to tear itself loose stuck just on the edge of release.

Tommy, her son, looked up at her from where he slumped against one wall. One hand was locked to his neck. His skin was deathly white, his gaze unseeing. His eyes were large and round, the orbs angled up towards the ceiling. She followed his gaze, tearing her own eyes away from him with an effort.

The hatch to the attic stood slightly open. As she watched, a dirty hand, almost black, reached around the edge and gently pulled it closed. Her scream came then as she backpedaled away from the scene.

She turned on her heel, nearly falling again as she ran towards her daughter's bedroom. She burst through the door, but Maxi was nowhere in sight.

Above the bed, the screen that sat high on one wall hung open, a dark square beyond. No! Her mind screamed. Her son was gone. Her daughter the same, or worse, taken? What could do such a thing? And where was her husband? The man who should have been looking after them this whole time?

Rita staggered from the room and into the one opposite.

Light from an outside streetlamp lit the room with dancing shadows. The covers on the bed were rumpled, disturbed, but she could still make out the shape underneath them. The sheets used to be white imported cotton. Now? Now they were mostly red as whatever lay underneath leaked fluid through them.

They lifted a little, deflated and lifted again. By the size, she knew it must be Mark. Rita grabbed the sheet and threw it from the bed, the sodden cover falling heavily to the floor. She thought she was done screaming. Thought that her world could not be brought down around her anymore. She was wrong.

Mark lay on the bed, his arms wide. The thing that lay underneath, curled next to him moved, as it was disturbed. It lifted its head and stared with startlingly human eyes. Opening its mouth, it hissed through teeth that were white in a dark, red-smeared face. Slowly it stood and cocked its head to one side, appraising her. Then it leapt with a growl, its hands shining silver with extra fingers of steel.

◆◆◆

The doctor looked at the little girl where she sat on the couch. Her eyes held a faraway look he had only seen on older people, survivors of killers and kidnappers. She hugged the headless doll closer to her chest. No amount of promises or placating could prise it from her grip.

He lifted a plain silver fob watch from the table and held it in his hand. He had used it many times before to help his patients. Regressing memories was a delicate business in adults, and in children even more so.

He swung it slowly backwards and forwards...backwards and forwards. Slowly, her eyes moved from the point she had been staring at and spotted the silver watch as it swayed. Her eyes started to tick left and right. Back again.

"That's right. It's a nice watch, isn't it?" He kept his voice low, calm. "Follow the watch, just the watch. It's all you can see." She was locked onto it now, the only thing in her world. Just as he wanted it to be.

"Your eyes seem heavy, maybe you need to sleep. Try to close your eyes now." His tone, low and purring, neutral and calming, was having the desired effect. He could see her eyes dripping lower, the hands holding the doll starting to relax, the head starting to drop towards her chest.

"You can't see it with your eyes anymore, but you can see it in your head. It's still moving side to side, left to right." She was almost fully under now. This was the time where he had to be careful. He knew that a child's mind was a fragile thing. He caught the watch on the backswing and lowered it silently back to the small table.

"Maxi? Can you hear me?" The little girl moved, a small shake of her head that he took for a nod of confirmation. He nodded along with her.

He knew what had happened, of course. Her parents and brother had been found in their home. Police had been called by a neighbor who heard noises coming from the property. On entering, they found the bodies of Rita, Mark and Tommy Barnes, all deceased. Maxi was found curled up in a cupboard in the kitchen, clutching the doll. She had not said a word since then. The police checked the house from top to bottom but found no-one else. The person responsible had fled.

The doctor leaned forward, staring at the top of the little girl's head. "Maxi, do you remember what happened?" The girl's head twitched as if in spasm, and he tensed, ready to pull her out of the trance if he needed to. "Maxi?"

Her head lifted slowly, and her eyes opened. The doctor sat back, his eyes widening at what he saw before him. Her lips were twisted into a smile, more a sneer. Maxi's eyes were narrowed and calculating, the personality that lurked behind them much older than her six years.

He tried again to get through. "Maxi, can you hear me?" She shook her head.

"Maxi is sleeping now." The voice was deeper, almost a growl.

He swallowed with a throat gone suddenly dry. "And what is your name? Who am I speaking to?"

The small head cocked to the side again, the grin spreading wider. "You can call me friend."

Sally's Ride

By Colt Henderson

Sally woke to a bright green light shining through her window. She sat up, rubbing the sleep from her eyes. Outside was a massive creature. When she looked out, she thought she must be dreaming. Despite the changes, she recognized her dog immediately.

"Dad, Roscoe is outside." Little Sally yelled down the hallway to her father's room.

Daniel met her at the master bedroom door with a look of exhaustion. "What, honey?"

"Roscoe was at my window. Well, he didn't really look like Roscoe because he was big. Real big, Dad, like humongous, and he was green. A bright green and he glowed, Daddy, he ..."

"Slow down, honey. Roscoe was lost when the nuclear plant melted down, remember?" Daniel took her hand, and they walked back down the hallway. When they got to the pink door, Daniel swung it open and stepped inside. Sally was right beside him, staring at the window. Both looked for the dog, but there was no sign of a green glowing canine. Daniel turned towards his daughter with a look she knew all too well. Before he even said a syllable, her eyes were welling up with tears.

"What have I told you about lying?"

"I swear, Daddy, I am not lying. It was Roscoe."

"I believe you, Little Bark. I am sure you were just having a dream."

"No, Daddy, it was real. I promise!" Sally stamped her feet and gave her dad a stern look.

"Ok," he laughed, which caused her to roll her eyes. "It could have walked off, right?"

"Sure." Sally slumped down and walked to her bed.

"Go back to sleep, and we will look for evidence in the morning."

"What!? Really?" Her pitch grew in disbelief.

"Of course. Love you, Little Bark."

"Love you too, Big Bark."

Sally settled in as she listened to her father's footsteps fade down the hall. She took one last look out the window and reached for the string of her lamp to turn out the light. After she got comfortable, it didn't take long to fall asleep.

Morning came, and Sally was up with the sun. She got herself breakfast and made sure her homework was in her backpack. Then she watched the clock, growing more impatient by the minute. Finally, she marched into his room, grabbed his foot, and tried to pull him out of bed.

"What are you doing?" Daniel grabbed the headboard at the last second.

"You promised we would look for evidence."

"Evidence ... of the dog, right?" Daniel replied as he sat up.

When he opened his eyes, Sally was standing inches from his face.

"Roscoe. It was Roscoe."

"You. Are. Too. Close," he said, staring back into her green eyes.

"It. Was. Roscoe," she replied before stepping back.

"Go get some breakfast, and I will be in there."

"I already ate, brushed my teeth, and got ready. Let's go!" she said as she turned around to show her pink backpack.

"Let me get dressed, and I will be out there."

"Okay."

Sally walked out of the room and into the kitchen, where she finished her glass of milk while she waited. Seven minutes later, as Sally watched the time on the microwave, Daniel walked in and opened the refrigerator. He pulled out a water bottle and looked at his daughter.

"Let's go," he said enthusiastically.

They marched out and around the house towards Sally's window. Once they got close, they could clearly see massive footprints in the dilapidated flower bed. Being a hunter, Daniel crouched down and examined the tracks. A few seconds later, he looked at Sally.

"There was something here, but it was bigger than Roscoe."

"It was Roscoe. He just grew."

"You were right, now lets get you to school."

A few hours passed, and Sally was at lunch with her friends. She was shocked when her dad appeared through the double doors of the cafeteria. He waved and continued over to the teacher. After a quick talk, Daniel started towards her with an expression she had seen only one other time, when her mom passed. Something was terribly wrong.

Daniel scooped her up and made his way out of the room. Sally waved goodbye to her friends. Once outside, she jumped down and tried to get answers. All she got was a vague description of a dog attack, and then Daniel went quiet. He was quiet the whole ride to a house a few streets down from theirs.

"Where are we?"

"Sally, I saw green, hairless, and deformed dogs attacking ... hurting people. This is serious. Stay in the truck. This is a friend, and we are picking her up. I will be right back."

Daniel jumped out and ran to the door. After ringing the doorbell, he started knocking. A flustered redhead opened up with a start, but once she recognized Daniel she tried to usher him in. He declined and then explained something. The woman's face went from happy, to confused, then to worried, but landed on scared as Daniel continued to talk.

In the distance, a howl crept into the air. Then the sky filled with howls, each one getting closer, until the sound surrounded them. Daniel and the redhead started running towards the truck, but something dark green ran from the back of the garage straight towards their fleeing ankles. Then another one from the other side of the street. Before Sally could do anything, different shades of green consumed the whole front yard of the house.

The ankle-biters hit them first. The redhead was the first to fall. That's when the slightly larger dogs approached. Daniel was able to launch a few of the monsters flying with well-timed kicks, but there were too many. Soon his feet were swarmed by the smallest of the green and hairless creatures.

As he battled the growing number and size of the dogs, the woman got mauled at the throat. The terrier's small but sharp teeth easily punctured the pale skin, causing blood to pour out around the pearl-white canines. Her arms had been attempting to push the dog away, but after the first cut her endurance slowly slipped away. Then her arms were bitten by the larger dogs that hungrily trotted up to the meal. With the number of mutated dogs growing, Sally could start to see the glow. It highlighted the scene of a woman being devoured by several dogs. Her gaze fell on her father's failing attempt to fight off the beasts. Unfortunately, there were just too many. Before he fell into the mound of dogs eating him, he motioned for Sally to flee, or at least that is what she thought.

Being in a small town, Daniel had let Sally drive his truck a few times around the property, so she scooted the seat all the way up, pressed the brake, and threw the truck into drive. She got several blocks before she ran into a bus and couldn't move anymore. Slamming the door open, she ran. She ran right into an intersection. Dogs appeared in front of her, so she turned, only to see more dogs. She spun around to find she was surrounded. She wet herself as she cried. When the dogs started to run, she crouched down in hopes of them leaving her alone. She listened as the hurried footsteps approached, only for a triumphant roar to stop them on a dime.

Sally looked up just as a hole started to form in the ring of dogs. A Rottweiler, the size of a cow, appeared out of nowhere. He had no fur, was covered in scars, and was bulging at every muscle. She could clearly see the glow on this monstrosity, and there was definitely something familiar about him. His eyes, shining brightly from the glow that escaped them as well, seemed to give her a knowing look. Still crouched down, Sally tried to close her eyes, but she felt like she was safe now, somehow.

"Roscoe?" she whispered.

As the beast slowly approached, Sally stood up. They were now face to face. The bright green glow from the hairless cow-sized dog consumed the little girl. He stepped within an inch of her face and started sniffing the surrounding air.

"Roscoe?"

The dog took a second to look her up and down and then licked her face, chin to forehead, which immediately started to melt. She cried out, but quickly covered her mouth to stifle the sound. With another victory sound, the dog turned around, and the pack followed him as he started to walk away from Sally. Once the massive leader got to the front, they broke out into a run towards the next town.

The February Pact

By R. A. King

Part 1

Chapter 1

The cold of February always got to Leah. She was never the type to enjoy the chill, and today it felt especially sharp. Snow blanketed the ground around her as she stood still, surrounded by family, their heads bowed low in grief. They all watched in silence, catching one last glimpse of the coffin as it was slowly lowered into the frozen earth.

Max had been unlucky for a long time. A string of misfortunes had led him here—his life ending in a tragic car crash that left the casket closed, leaving memories to fill in the blanks.

Leah exhaled, her breath curling into the air like smoke. She watched as the casket settled at the bottom of the grave and a strange discomfort arose within her. The distance between her and the others suddenly felt too wide. She stepped forward, crunching through the snow.

"Mom?" she called gently, her voice catching.

Her mother turned, eyes red-rimmed but soft, giving her a silent nod to speak.

"Why does someone always die in February?" Leah asked. Her mother blinked, surprised. "What—what do you mean?"

"This is the third year in a row."

Her mother paused, her expression thoughtful, then said quietly, "That's just how it is, sweetheart. We don't get to choose when it's someone's time."

Leah stood there, stunned into silence. A knot formed in her chest and her eyes stung.

"Oh, come here," her mom said, pulling her into a hug. Leah leaned into it. It was exactly what she needed, but the unease lingered. The hug brought warmth, but not comfort.

They separated when it was time to go. Leah trudged through the snow toward the car, but halfway there she stopped. She turned back toward the grave, her voice low but firm.

"Every year, one of us goes. But not me. Not this time."

She turned again and kept walking, slipping into the car. The door slammed shut, and moments later the vehicle disappeared onto the snow-covered roads, leaving behind only tire tracks and the sound of the wind.

Chapter 2

Leah couldn't let it go. The pattern gnawed at her. February. Every year. Always someone from the Harrow side. It wasn't just a coincidence, it couldn't be. She cleared her desk and spread out everything she could find: old obituaries, family photo albums, scribbled dates and names. Red ink circled year after year. Great-Aunt Ellen, 2003. Cousin Paul, 2008. Her dad, 2022. Max, now. A string of deaths like beads on a cursed thread. Always February. Always blood. But no answers.

Her grandmother's attic had always creeped her out with its sloped ceiling and the way light slanted through the slats, dust hanging like cobwebs in the air. Still, something told her that if answers existed, they'd be here. She climbed the narrow stairs, the boards creaking beneath her feet.

Boxes surrounded her like forgotten tombstones. Faded labels, cracked tape, and old fabric draped over corners like shrouds. She picked through carefully, setting aside things that felt too fragile, until one chest in the corner caught her eye. Cedar, old but solid. The latch was broken.

Inside were wrapped linens, yellowed paper, and old family keepsakes. She lifted out a bundle of letters, brittle with age. Beneath that, something heavier. A journal. She sat back on her heels, cradling it in her hands. The name inside, written in ink that had bled just slightly with time: Edmund Harrow, 1847. The air in the attic felt colder.

She opened the journal and Edmund's voice whispered up from the past, stiff and formal, the lines pressed deep into the paper.

The frost has not lifted for weeks. Livestock failing. Stores near gone. Margaret coughs at night—she is fading.

The pages crackled as she turned them. Each entry darker than the last:

We went to the Hollow. Spoke the names. Drew the circle.

She stopped and read that line again.

We called it from the Hollow, and it answered. In voice and mirror. One life, each February, for what we asked.

Her fingers tightened on the journal. The attic groaned softly around her.

More entries followed; frenzied, scattered, written with uneven slashes of ink. Descriptions of voices in the wind, of something that watched from mirrors, that waited in stone. Then a sketch. A circle of stones with connecting lines, like a ritual diagram, and below it, a map, rough but familiar. A creek. A bluff. An "X" marked near the woods with the words hollow gate scratched beside it.

Leah stared at it, her heart pounding. She knew that place. Behind the old church, where the forest thickened and the air always felt colder, even in summer.

She looked back at the final scrawl.

We still owe it. The stone must be fed, or we pay more dearly. The Harrow line bears the weight. The promise was blood, and so it shall be.

She closed the journal slowly, her hands trembling.

Chapter 3

The snow was falling again when Leah set out, the world hushed beneath a gray sky. She followed the crude map from Edmund's journal, each landmark a breadcrumb leading deeper into the woods. The crooked bend of the creek, the leaning trees, the old fence posts lost in undergrowth—they were all still there, just as he'd drawn them in 1847.

Her boots crunched through the snow as she pushed through tangled brambles, heart pounding. After what felt like hours, the trees suddenly parted, revealing a clearing absorbed in silence. At its center stood the ruins of a chapel, what was left of one, anyway. The stone walls were half-collapsed, draped in ivy and rimed with frost. The roof was long gone, and snow fell freely inside. It looked like it had been forgotten for centuries, but the ground felt strangely undisturbed, like time had curled around this place without touching it.

Leah stepped forward, drawn to the circle of stones nestled in the clearing. They were worn smooth with age, arranged in a perfect ring, and somehow untouched by snow. Kneeling beside one, she reached out, expecting the chill of stone. But the surface was warm. Not just warm, alive. Like something was beneath it, breathing slowly and deeply.

A whisper cut through the stillness.

"Leah..."

She froze. The voice was soft, familiar.

"Leah..."

Max.

She stumbled backward, eyes wide. The whisper came again, barely audible but unmistakably his. It was the way he used to call her name when he was about to sneak up on her—playful, teasing. Only now it felt wrong. Like someone trying to sound like him. There was no one around, just the empty woods, the crumbling chapel, the warm stones, and that voice threading through the air.

She turned and ran. Branches clawed at her coat, snow kicked up around her boots as she fled the clearing. The whisper followed her for a time, then faded into the wind. She didn't stop until she reached the edge of the woods, lungs burning, her face damp with sweat despite the cold.

That night, sleep came fitfully. When she finally drifted off, the dream took her back to the clearing, but it was different. No snow, no cold, just a strange silver light soaking everything in a dim glow. She stood at the edge of the stone ring, and across from her, something stood inside of it.

It looked like her. Same clothes. Same build. Same hair tumbling from the hood of her coat. But the way it moved, delayed, unnatural, sent ice through her veins. Its smile came half a second too late. Its eyes were too dark, swallowing the light instead of reflecting it.

She tried to move, to step back, but her limbs felt heavy. The figure lifted a hand. So did she. For a moment, they were mirrors. Then it stepped forward, out of sync, and the illusion shattered.

Leah couldn't move. The figure cocked its head, mimicking her curiosity or mocking it, she couldn't tell. It raised a hand again, curling its fingers into a slow, deliberate fist. She felt her chest tighten, like something was squeezing her heart.

She woke up gasping, drenched in sweat, tangled in the sheets as if they were vines. Her room was silent, but her skin crawled. Across the room the mirror on her dresser caught her eye. Her reflection stared back. Still, watchful. Too still.

Leah got up and turned the mirror to face the wall, hands trembling. She didn't sleep again that night. She couldn't stop thinking about the thing in the clearing. The thing that wore her face.

Chapter 4

Leah's heart raced as she stood in front of her grandfather's door. She tried to prepare herself for this moment, but standing there now, the weight of what she was about to ask settled heavily in her chest. She knocked firmly, and after a moment, the door creaked open.

Her grandfather stood in the doorway, his tired eyes squinting against the light. His hair had thinned, and his back was hunched, but his gaze held a sharpness that made Leah's stomach tighten.

"Leah," he rasped, his voice rough. "Come in."

She didn't move. "I need to talk to you. Now."

The brief flicker of something unreadable in his eyes—Regret? Fear?—was gone in an instant. He stepped aside, nodding for her to enter. "Sit."

Leah stepped into the dimly lit room, taking in the familiar scent of old books, leather, and the faint trace of tobacco. The fire crackled softly in the hearth, casting flickering shadows on the walls. She took a seat, her hands trembling in her lap, and waited.

After a long silence, her grandfather finally spoke, his voice low. "What do you know?"

Leah clenched her fists, taking a steadying breath. "I know about Edmund. About the pact."

Her grandfather's face tightened, and for a moment she thought he might close up entirely. But then he exhaled slowly, his gaze distant, and sank into his chair with a heavy sigh. "I figured you'd find out eventually," he muttered. "You've always been too damn curious for your own good."

She leaned forward, trying to steady the whirlwind in her chest. "Tell me everything. I need to know."

He hesitated, rubbing his face as if trying to wipe away the years of guilt and shame. Finally, he spoke, his voice barely above a whisper. "Edmund Harrow made a deal. A blood pact with something beneath the ground. Something old. Something that... that could give us power. Protect us from the misfortune that haunted our line."

Leah's breath caught. "What kind of power?"

His eyes shifted, darkening with regret. "The kind that comes with a price. One life every year. A sacrifice. Always in February. It was a way to protect the family, to keep us safe from the things that would destroy us. But the price... the price was steep."

Leah's stomach dropped as the realization sank in. "So... every year, someone dies. Someone from the family."

Her grandfather nodded, his eyes hollow. "It can't be broken. Only paid."

She paused, her throat dry. "And... and you've just... accepted it?"

His gaze hardened, but there was sadness there too. "For a long time, we drew names. We knew who would go. It wasn't easy, but we had control. Now... now it's different. The deaths don't follow the pattern anymore. They happen at random. It's as if the... thing we made the pact with doesn't care about the rules anymore."

Leah's mind raced, the weight of the revelation pressing on her chest. "What if we just... stop it? What if no one dies this year?"

Her grandfather's face went pale, and for a moment he looked like he might tell her to leave, to forget this conversation ever happened. But he didn't. Instead, his voice dropped to a whisper, laden with fear. "Then it comes to collect."

Leah's blood ran cold. "What does that mean?"

His gaze met hers, and the fear in his eyes was enough to make her heart skip a beat. "It means you don't want to know. If the pact isn't paid, it comes for more than just one life. It takes what it's owed, no matter the cost."

The room fell silent. Leah couldn't move, couldn't breathe. The air felt thick, as though the walls themselves were closing in around her. She opened her mouth, but no words came out.

"Leah," her grandfather said, his voice barely audible, "we're trapped. And there's no way out."

Chapter 5

The days after her conversation with her grandfather were filled with unease, like something stalking her from the shadows just beyond her line of sight. She could feel it always there, following her movements, a breath on her neck. The house seemed quieter than usual, as if the walls themselves were holding their breath.

The lights flickered in the corner of her eye when she tried to play music, the faint hum of the speakers warping and distorting into something that didn't belong. At night, when she passed by mirrors, she could swear they fogged up from the inside. A breath, slow and steady, as though someone was watching her, waiting.

She tried to push it all away. She tried to focus on her work and her studies, but every time she glanced into a reflective surface, the unease crept back. And every night, her dreams became darker and more vivid.

February 27th arrived, and the air was thick with dread. Leah stood in front of the mirror that morning, trying to gather the courage to face the day. She paused, hand resting on the bathroom counter. She stared at her reflection as if willing it to stay still, to prove she was in control.

But it didn't. Her reflection grinned, a slow, sinister smile that stretched wider than hers ever did. Her pulse quickened, but she didn't move. The smile lingered. Her chest tightened as she paused, trying to keep the rising panic at bay.

"Stop it," she whispered to the glass.

But the reflection didn't stop. It tilted its head to the side, as though mocking her, then smirked wider. That's when Leah knew. She couldn't run anymore. The Hollow One had come. It was time to face it.

By the time evening rolled around, Leah was prepared. She had gathered the things she would need: rope, candles, the journal. She had studied the journal again, trying to understand the dark words Edmund had written so many years ago. His warnings, his instructions, were maddeningly cryptic, but there was one thing that stood out—the name. The name that was never fully written out, just hinted at in a line of barely legible script. Leah had pieced it together. It was the key to ending it.

She shoved the journal into her bag and made her way toward the woods, the cold air biting at her skin. The moon hung low in the sky, barely visible through the swirling clouds. It was a perfect night to confront what had haunted her family for generations.

Chapter 6

The faint glow of the stones illuminated the clearing, their ancient surfaces pulsing softly, as if they had come alive after all these years.

The wind was still, but the air around Leah felt charged, like electricity humming beneath the surface. The candles flickered and cast long, eerie shadows on the snow-covered ground. The fog that had settled around the chapel began to swirl in on itself, twisting and curling like something alive.

Then, through the mist, a figure emerged. At first, it seemed like Leah herself—her height, her shape, her every feature exactly the same. But as the fog parted, Leah felt the air grow colder, the atmosphere thick with a malevolent presence.

This version of her, the doppelgänger, had an unnatural quality. Its hair floated as though weightless, trailing behind it like something underwater. Its eyes were hollow, dark pits that seemed to suck in the light, and its smile, her smile, was far too wide, stretching impossibly across its face.

The world seemed to stop, Leah's heart hammering in her chest. She didn't move. She couldn't.

The figure took a step forward, its feet barely disturbing the fog that surrounded it. "You always come," the creature said, its voice a twisted mimicry of Leah's own, soft and haunting. "You always choose."

Leah's mind raced. What was this? What was standing in front of her? It looked like her, but it couldn't be her. It was something else, something ancient, something that wore her face like a mask.

The doppelgänger tilted its head, the movement slow, deliberate, as if savoring her confusion. "Did you think you were the first?" it asked. "Did you think you were the only one who has tried to end it?"

Leah paused, trying to find her voice. "What are you?" Her voice sounded small, too fragile in the heavy, damp air.

"I am you," the figure replied, its smile growing wider, stretching beyond what any human face should be capable of. "I am every one of you. I've been you for generations." The words echoed in the air, as though reverberating from deep within the earth. "I am the one who stays. The one who becomes the tether."

Leah stepped back, legs trembling. The fog seemed to close in on her as the figure moved closer, its feet barely touching the ground, gliding instead of walking. "No," Leah said, her voice firmer now. "This isn't possible."

The figure tilted its head again, its hair flowing in an invisible wind. "You don't believe me?" It laughed a low, hollow sound that seemed to rattle the surrounding air. "Your family's bloodline has been tethered to the Hollow One for centuries. Edmund was only the first. Each one of you is part of the cycle. Each one of you chooses."

Leah felt the weight of its words settle on her chest, cold and suffocating. "What do you mean? What do you mean 'chooses'?"

"You choose to live, and in doing so, you choose who will die." The figure's eyes locked onto Leah's, and for a moment she felt as though it was seeing right through her, peeling back every layer of her soul. "And when the time comes, when there is no more choice... you choose to stay. To become the tether. To keep the debt alive. To become part of the cycle."

Leah recoiled, horror clawing at her insides. "The tether?"

The figure's smile never wavered. "To stop the debt, one must stay. One must become the tether." It stepped forward again, its voice growing softer, more insistent. "It's the only way to break the cycle. Only one can escape. But it's never the one who calls. It's the one who stays."

Leah's pulse quickened. She had no words. She felt the weight of everything, of the lives lost, of the family bound to this dark pact, of the generations trapped in an endless loop of sacrifice and survival.

"But," Leah started, her voice shaking, "what if no one chooses? What if... what if I don't?"

The doppelgänger smiled wider, its eyes dark pits of nothingness. "Then it comes. The Hollow One will come to claim what is owed. It's already watching, already hungry." The figure reached out, its fingers cold as ice, brushing lightly against Leah's cheek. "And when it comes, it will take more than one life. It will take everything."

Leah's mind spun as the figure's words twisted through her thoughts. She could feel the coldness of its touch lingering on her skin. It was right. She had no choice. There was no way out. The debt had been paid for generations, and no matter what she did, it would continue until someone stayed, until someone gave their life to keep it from coming for more.

The figure took another step closer, its eyes unblinking, its smile stretched too wide. "You've always known this."

Leah's heart hammered in her chest as the truth settled around her. She had been running from this moment, but now, standing face-to-face with the thing that wore her face, she understood. To stop it, to end it, someone had to stay. Someone had to become the tether. And there was no way out.

Chapter 7

The stones glowed with a sickly white light, brighter now, pulsing as the ritual locked into place. Leah stood inside the ancient circle, symbols traced in air and earth around her, the candlelight flickering wildly in the gale that had risen from nowhere. Fog churned around her feet like restless spirits. And across from her, within the trap, stood the thing that wore her face.

Her mirror-self, the Hollow One's vessel, grinned, its eyes empty and unblinking. Hair floated unnaturally, as if underwater. Its smile stretched far too wide.

"I'm not choosing," Leah said, voice raw from shouting the ritual words. "No more deaths. No more deals."

"You think this ends it? You think you've won?" Its voice flickered between tones, mocking, pleading, cold. "You can still trade places. Spare them all. Just one life. Yours."

Temptation dripped from every word. It would be so easy. Step into the reflection. Take the burden herself. Everyone else would be safe.

But she remembered Edmund's journal. The drawings of circles. The trembling script of his confession and the lives that had already been taken, three Februaries in a row, and countless more before that. Her cousin Max. Her aunt. Her great-grandfather. All to feed this thing.

Leah lifted her hand, traced the final mark mid-air, and let the last word fall from her lips like a stone. The circle erupted in a sharp, blinding pulse of light. The doppelgänger shrieked, high-pitched, inhuman. It twisted within the boundary, its form unraveling in flashes. Its grin faltered for the first time.

"No!" it howled, voice breaking into dozens. "You can't do this! You don't understand!" But Leah didn't flinch. She held the circle. The stones dimmed. The fog pulled inward, folding in on itself. And the mirror-Leah was gone. Only the ring of stones remained, charred at the edges, cold now. The air, once tight and buzzing, felt empty. Hollow.

Leah collapsed to her knees, heart still hammering. Blood streaked her palms where the journal's pages had cut her. Her breath fogged out in bursts, though the woods had gone unnaturally still.

When dawn crept through the trees, pale and gold, she rose to her feet and walked away from the ruined circle, exhausted, bloodied, unsure if what she'd done had worked.

Chapter 8

Weeks passed. The cold of February gave way to the slow thaw of March. Leah didn't speak about what had happened. Not to her mother. Not to the others. She still had the journal, now locked in a box beneath her bed. The stones were silent. The woods were quiet. Nothing had come for anyone else.

But she didn't sleep well. Every creak of the floor made her heart jolt. Every mirror she passed made her look twice. She couldn't forget the final words: *You don't understand.*

One afternoon, the house was quiet. Her little brother, Caleb, padded down the hallway, dragging a toy truck behind him. Leah sat on the couch, head heavy with sleep, a forgotten book in her lap. Somewhere, the dishwasher hummed.

She didn't notice Caleb turn into the bathroom. Didn't hear the door creak open. Inside, the light was soft, golden through the window. The mirror above the sink reflected the small boy's round face as he stood on tiptoe to peer into the glass.

He tilted his head.

His reflection tilted back.

Then it smiled.

The Girl with the Flowered Bonnet

By Sharon D. Ballentine

Part 1

Three motionless kids stared at the three kids looking down on them from a painting that hung on the wall in their family room.

"I don't know how Mom thinks they remind her of us. I wouldn't be caught dead in clothes like those," the oldest boy, Jason, said.

"Me either," Carl, the youngest boy, agreed. "I mean. They're nerds. Does that mean Mom thinks we are nerds?"

"You are a nerd," Jason said.

"Shut up, jerk."

"I wouldn't be caught dead in those clothes."

"I'd wear what the little girl has on. It's cute. She's cute. She looks like one of my dolls. I'm going to call her Flower, like the flowers on her bonnie."

"Bonnet," Jason corrected her.

"Girls don't wear outfits like that anymore either, like boys don't wear short pants," Carl said.

"I wear gym shorts."

"Whatever. Do you wear short pantsuits and long socks to be dressed up?"

"The girl looks cute."

"You said that," Carl said.

"Stop being a jerk," Jason said.

The dog sat in the doorway of the family room.

"Anyway," Carl said. "They're creepy."

"You read too many creepy books. It's all in your mind."

"No, no," Carl said to his older brother. "They're staring at us."

The dog barked.

"What's with him?" Carl asked. He turned around and looked at the dog, Phoenix.

"I want a bonnie like hers."

"It's a bonnet. Come on squirt, let's go get breakfast," Jason said as he picked up his five-year-old sister. The little girl, Carrie, stared at the little girl in the picture with the bonnet on her head as her brother carried her from the room. Carl trailed them.

Carrie waved as they walked out of the room. The little girl in the portrait stared at them as they left the room. The dog growled at the picture and followed the kids down the hall.

"Phoenix doesn't like the painting either," Carl said.

"Phoenix doesn't like anyone but us. That's her job," Jason said.

"Mom," Carrie said to her mother, "can I have a bonnie, like the little girl in the picture?"

"May I have," her mother corrected her.

"Bonnet," Jason corrected her. "She wants a bonnet like the little girl in the painting."

"You think that painting is valuable?" the father asked his wife. "The artwork is good. The kids look life-like."

"Possibly," she replied, "but I'm not sure I want to sell it. It looks nice in the family room."

"Don't sell it," said Carrie. "I like it. I like the little girl. We can have playdates."

"You can't have playdates with a picture," Carl said.

"I can too! Can't I, Mom?"

Their mother smiled. "And I'll find you a bonnet like hers, and you can invite your little friends over for tea too."

"We won't sell it, kitten," her father said.

Carrie smiled. Her brothers rolled their eyes in big-brother tolerance.

•••

The grandfather clock in the hallway struck 3 a.m. Everyone in the house was asleep, including Phoenix. The gong of the clock never bothered them. They were accustomed to its deep voice sounding nighttime peace and tranquility.

In the family room, the eyes of the kids in the painting moved. They peered into the quiet, dark room.

"I like her," a soft voice whispered into the darkness.

"I don't," another voice replied. "My clothes are not ugly. His are."

"None we have met wear clothes like ours."

"The little girl wants a bonnet with flowers like mine. We can be sisters. We can play together."

"We're not here to play, and you are not a child. This is the third family. The third family will break the spell, and we can be free."

"If we have to hurt the little girl, I don't want to be free. I want to play with her."

"You are over a hundred years old."

"I shall play with that little boy who talked about my pants. I shall play with him like he has never been played with before."

"But you cannot kill him or he is no good to us. Well, not until the time is right. Then he will die."

The dog, who was sleeping in his bed in the boys' room, heard the voices. He barked.

"Be quiet, Phoenix," one of the boys said, as he turned over in his bed. "It's just the clock, and you know it."

The dog whined, but he didn't go back to sleep. He lowered his head between his front paws, and his watchful eyes stared into the darkened room.

◆◆◆

Friday evening after school, Jason and Carl played a video game in the family room. Lights from the game flashed across their faces. Voices yelled and weapons blasted and flared as the boys conquered some evil demon.

Carrie sat at her little table wearing a pink princess dress, pink gloves, and a crown on her head. Her dolls and a bear occupied the other chairs at her table. She talked to them about a make-believe party she was going to have Saturday.

"The Queen of Snowflakes will be here. I'm wearing my fairy dress and bonnet if Mom finds me a bonnet in time for the party. If not, we can have the party next weekend."

"What?" she asked one of her dolls. "Yes, maybe she can find one for both of you. Don't worry, Teddy, you'll be dressed appropriately. Bears don't wear bonnets. One just has to be dressed appropriately for the queen. Your bowtie will go quite well." She held her head up and stuck her nose in the air. "Wouldn't you agree, Juliet?"

"Juliet!" Carl said as lights from the Playstation flashed across his face. "Who's Juliet?"

"It's the little girl in the picture. That's what I call her, Juliet. Juliet is a pretty name for a pretty little girl with a bonnet on her head."

"Juliet killed herself in a play we're reading at school," Carl said. "Because she saw her boyfriend dead because he killed himself because he thought she was dead, but she wasn't. She was just sleeping."

"Don't talk to her about stories like that," Jason said.

"What's kill herself mean?"

"Die! Die!" Carl yelled as he frantically manipulated his way through the game.

"She's not dead."

"Is too," Carl replied.

"You don't know anything! She smiles at me sometimes. Dead can't do that."

"Oh, brother!" The lights of the game continued flashing on his face.

Carry got up from the table, walked over to her brothers, and handed them her phone. "Take a picture of me in front of the painting. Wait! Wait! Let me stand on the side where the girl is."

"We're busy," Carl said.

"Here. I'll do it," Jason said. He put down the controller.

"You're just doing that because you're losing."

"I'm doing it because I don't want to embarrass you. Look again. I'm about to corner you." Jason took the phone from his little sister and got up. "Pause the game. I've got to get a drink anyway, and you can study how I'm about to whip your butt."

Carrie posed in front of the painting and smiled happily.

After he snapped a couple of pictures, Jason handed Carrie her phone and turned to walk out of the room. Phoenix looked at him, but he did not move from his position in the doorway. Jason stepped over the dog, paused, and said, "What's up with Phoenix?"

"I don't know. He's been acting weird."

"It's that painting. I don't think he likes it."

"I don't like it much either."

The kids in the painting frowned. Phoenix growled.

♦♦♦

The grandfather clock in the hallway gonged three times. It was a slow, measured, throaty sound that echoed throughout the house but disturbed no one. The house was asleep and dark except for the soft glow of strategically placed night lights.

One of the boys in the picture whispered. "No one is near. Everyone is asleep. Even that horrible animal." He stepped out of the painting onto the family room floor. The two other kids followed.

The little girl in the flowered bonnet went immediately to where Carrie had sat hours before, talking to her dolls and bear about what they were planning to wear at the make-believe tea party. The girl sat in Carrie's seat, but she was alone at the table because Carrie had taken her dolls and bears with her when she left the room.

One of the boys from the painting stared at the Playstation. "What did they do to make this thing come alive?" he asked.

"Don't touch it," the other boy from the painting said. "The thing was loud when they woke it. They will hear it and return."

The little girl with the flowered bonnet on her head poured imaginary tea for herself and the two dolls and bear who weren't there. "How many lumps of sugar, madam?" she asked. "And for you, madam? How about you, Sir Bear? Who would like cream? Oh, yes," she continued talking to the absent dolls and bear, "I would love to come to your tea party, Carrie. What would be appropriate for me to wear?" She pretended to ask Carrie, who was in her bed asleep. "I know my bonnet is appropriate. You love it, but what about the rest of my attire? It is not fitting to attend an audience with the queen, but is it acceptable to you? I'm afraid it is all that I have. Perhaps you would be good enough to let me borrow one of your beautiful gowns?"

The boy not in front of the PlayStation said, "We must stop all this foolishness. We must talk about what to do next."

"I don't want to," the little girl said.

"But we must," the boy in front of the PlayStation said.

"Yes," the other boy agreed. "It is the way we must follow, and it is the final time. We must do it without error, else we shall have to do it again and again."

"Yes, but the other kids before we arrived here had been so horrid. I did not care what happened to them at all," the girl with the bonnet on her head said.

"That boy talked about my pants," the boy at the Playstation said.

"I did not like that either, but he did not call us names or talk about our faces and how we look. Our clothes are strange to them as are theirs to us. We have witnessed how clothes are different over time. I do not fault him for that."

"The girl likes my bonnet, and she said her mother was going to get her one too, and she is having a tea party, and I am invited. I want to go to the tea party. I want to stay here in this house forever. I want her to be my little sister! But the truth of the matter is that we are trapped here. I warned you to be cautious of that witch and her daughter!" She stared at the boy who was standing.

"The witch was going to kill me! Besides, this little girl that you like so much will not be little forever. She will grow into a woman and leave this house, and we will be stuck in this house."

"Because of what you did to the witch's daughter!" the boy at the Playstation yelled. He slammed his hand onto the controller. The game came to life.

Noise filled the room. The girl jumped up from the table and upset the table setting.

Phoenix, Jason, and Carl heard the noise. Phoenix howled. Lights came on in the hallway. The parents entered the hallway just as the boys opened the door to their bedroom and rushed towards the family room.

"Did you boys forget to turn off that video game?" their father asked.

"No," Jason replied. He turned the light on in the family room. The family room was calm, but the lights in the video game were flashing.

"You must have," Jason said to Carl. "The game just doesn't come on by itself."

Carrie stepped from behind her brothers. Her father picked her up. She wiped her eyes and said, "That's not the way I left my table."

The three kids in the painting stared out into the room. Carl said, "I don't like those kids."

Phoenix barked and backed away.

PART 2

"Look at this," Carrie said as she handed her phone to Jason.

He took her phone, stared at it, and said, "Okay, so you look cute."

"No, that's not what I'm talking about. The little girl is looking down in the picture. She's looking at me."

"No way. You're weird," Carl said. He snatched the phone from Jason's hand, plopped down on the bed beside his brother, and the three huddled to study the picture.

"That's weird. It does look like it," Jason said.

"You're crazy. That's just the way it looks," Carl said. "Let's go look at her."

They marched down the hall. The dog followed. When they reached the family room, Phoenix remained in the hall. The three kids stood in the middle of the room and stared at the picture on the phone and then at the painting.

"It does look like it, doesn't it?"

"Maybe," Jason said to Carl, "but I think it's just the way the light is on the painting. The lights are playing tricks, that's all." He handed the phone back to Carrie. He turned and walked out of the room. Carrie, Carl, and Phoenix trailed him down the hall. Phoenix growled.

Carrie asked Phoenix, "What's wrong, boy?"

Phoenix looked up at her with bright eyes and a big dog smile.

The grandfather clock gonged 4am. Carl climbed out of his bed quietly so as not to wake his brother. He opened the door silently and tiptoed down the hall, his bare feet quiet on the hardwood floor. He paused just before he reached the doorway. The clock struck its final note. He stopped just before he reached the family room and listened.

"It's a night away, unless you capture the little girl's soul we will all be locked in the portrait forever."

"But I like her," the girl with the flowered bonnet on her head protested.

One of the boys replied, "You can stay in the portrait and like her from the portrait forever, or you can change places with her before tomorrow ends and live. There are no other choices."

The little girl with the bonnet on her head pouted.

"So, let us review the steps to make the switch happen. There can be no mistakes."

Carl tiptoed back to his room. His hands were shaking, and sweat was popping out from his face, though he'd never admit it to anyone. He quietly opened the door to his bedroom and entered. Phoenix popped his head. Carl shook Jason awake.

"What now?" Jason asked groggily.

"I was right. Their eyes did look different. That's not just a painting. They're kids like us, I think, but they are somehow locked in that painting, and they want to change places with us and trap us, so they can get out. Come on, but you've got to be quiet, and you can hear them for yourself. They're talking right, but Phoenix has got to stay in here because he'll growl. He might even attack, and who knows what will happen then. He never liked that painting in the first place. That's why he won't go in the room and he growls all the time at it. Dogs see things. Dogs know things we don't. Come on. You'll see for yourself."

The clock gonged 12am. Everyone was asleep except the two boys and Phoenix.

The next morning, the family sat at the breakfast table.

"Can I have more jelly on my toast?" Carrie asked.

"May I have more jelly on my toast?" her mother corrected her.

"Yes, you can have some more too," Carrie replied innocently.

They all laughed as her mother spread more jelly on her toast.

Jason asked, "Mom, what do you know about that painting in the family room?"

"Not much. It isn't signed, which makes it unusual. But it's a good painting. So lifelike. The details, the strokes, the colors. The kids almost seem alive."

Their father said, "I noticed that too. I was in there reading, and it seemed like they were looking at me when I looked up. It's a good painting. You should get more for it than you paid."

"You think?"

"Where did you say it came from?" Jason continued.

"Are you into antiques now?" his father asked.

"Maybe," Jason replied.

"At an estate sale," their mother said, "on 43rd and Eldridge Road. An old couple died. They'd been living in the house all their lives. I understand the painting had been passed down for generations and was painted by one of their ancestors. It has never been outside their family, until now."

"What do you know about the family, anything?" Carl asked.

"What's up with you two? I didn't realize you were so into art," their mother asked.

"Just wondering," Jason replied.

"Isn't that one of the families that's been around since this was a little one-horse town?" their mother asked. "But they weren't born here. They moved from somewhere in the east."

"I think you're right," their father continued. "I heard that their family can be traced back to the pilgrims. I heard people say. It's a couple other families like them in that area. Old families."

"What's a pilgrim?" Carrie asked.

"Just really religious people from a long time ago," Carl interjected. "They burned women at the stake."

"Why didn't they burn the men's steaks too?" Carrie asked.

"No, burned ..."

"That's enough," their mother interrupted.

"We're going out tonight," their father said. "You guys can stay up late. It's not a school night."

"Yehhh!" Carrie cheered.

"Late for you is 8 o'clock," Jason said.

"I will stay up late tonight," Carrie replied. "You'll see. I'll stay up very late. I'm having a party with the queen."

◆◆◆

Music from the boys' room followed Carrie down the hall. She was smiling because she was happy with her pink princess dress that matched her new bonnet that her mother had bought her. She walked confidently in her little plastic slippers. Carrie was sure that they looked like Cinderella's glass slippers. She cuddled her two dolls and bear in her arms lovingly, along with a bag of cookies. Phoenix followed her. He walked reluctantly, but he loved her as much as she loved her dolls.

He went wherever Carrie went. The gonging of the grandfather clock marked each of her little steps. Outside, thunder grumbled.

Phoenix reached the doorway to the family room. He stopped and growled, as was his usual habit since the portrait had been hung in the room. Carrie stopped as well. The little girl with the flowered bonnet on her head sat at Carrie's little table.

"Come play with me," the little girl with the flowered bonnet said. She was smiling. Her smile was innocent and sincere and pretty.

In their bedroom, Carl said to Jason, "I know I'm not crazy. Look at this picture I took of Carrie standing under the painting. The kids in the painting are all looking one way. Now look at the one I took later when I was in there by myself. They weren't expecting me. Look at the boys, their eyes are looking at me, but the girl isn't. The boys are frowning at me."

Carrie stepped into the family room cautiously. The little girl with the flowered bonnet said, "We must be ready for the tea party with the queen. Sit down. We must make plans." She smiled happily. "What shall we serve?"

Carrie took another step towards the little girl.

"It's okay," the little girl with the flowered bonnet said. "We're friends. You've got a bonnet like mine, but I think yours is prettier." Carrie took another step towards the table. She looked at the painting. The little boys were in the painting. They looked like they always did. "Don't worry about them. We can sit and talk and have make-believe tea and cakes. We can get to know each other." She picked up a teacup and pretended to sip from it.

"I brought cookies," Carrie said. Carrie took another step towards the table. "How are you out of the picture? You're make-believe like the tea party and the queen."

"No, I am not. I am real, and I want to be with you. We can play together. No one plays tea with me, and no one plays with you, but we can play together. Always."

"Always?" Carrie stopped walking towards the table. "My daddy says nothing is always. I heard him say that."

"He did not mean the bond that ties two sisters together. We can be sisters."

"But you are not real. We are not sisters. I have no sisters. I have two brothers. I know the difference between real and not real."

"Then how could you be talking to me if I am not real? Come closer. Touch me and you will see."

Carrie did not move. The clock sounded its last gong. Phoenix howled and bared his teeth. Jason and Carl ran down the hall towards the family room.

The little girl with the flowered bonnet on her head got up from the table and started walking towards Carrie. "Here, let me help you. It will be easy. We shall be sisters forever." She held out her hand towards Carrie.

"No, Carrie!" Jason and Carl yelled at the same time as they rushed into the room. Jason grabbed Carrie up into his arms with her dolls, bear, and cookies. "This is stranger danger. You don't go near strangers. You don't even talk to strangers."

The boys in the portrait jumped down and turned into two old men. "Let her go!" one of the men demanded.

Jason stepped backwards. Carrie held tight to her dolls and bear and squeezed her cookies into crumbs.

Phoenix came into the room for the first time. He stood between the two men from the painting and his family. His hackles were up. He bared his teeth, and he growled and barked like a wild beast.

One of the men said, "It is not our intention to bring harm to the little girl. We need her help to free us."

It was as if Phoenix understood the men's intention. The dog moved closer to the men, his hackles up, his paws solid on the floor, his teeth bared viciously.

"Remove that beast!" one of the men demanded.

Jason moved backward again. "You will no way move past him. You will not take my little sister from my arms. If you could have, you would have by now. She has to come willingly, and I am her will because she is too small to understand will and its consequences."

"You must understand. We wish her no harm, but we are trapped in that painting and there is but one way out, and that time has come, and she, who you hold in your arms, is the way."

"You see, we made a mistake," the other man said. "We, as children, had no one to take guard of our lives. We were abandoned children, alone, and no one warned us to beware of the dangerous thing we were doing. We were playing with the little girl of a witch, and we accidentally killed her."

"Yes, it was an accident. We didn't mean to hurt her, but witches care not whether a thing is accidental or not. So we need the little girl you hold in your arms to give life to the spirit of the witch's daughter, there." They point to the little girl at the table with the flowered bonnet on her head.

"And then we can be free." One of the men started to move towards Jason. Phoenix stood his ground in front of Jason and Carrie and her dolls and her bear. He growled viciously.

One of the men moved towards Phoenix. "I shall squeeze the life from this beast."

"While I snatch that child from your arms, there is nothing you can do to stop it! You are but a child!" the other man said.

But no one was paying attention to Carl. Carl rushed towards the little girl with the flowered bonnet on her head. He snatched the bonnet from the little girl's head.

The two men in the picture howled in agony. "No! No! You do not know what it is you do!"

The two men were snatched back into the painting as if they had been grabbed by invisible hands. When they entered the painting, they became young boys again, in short pants suits and long socks. They were frozen in place and silent.

"Yeah, I know what I'm doing," Carl yelled. Thunder outside the house roared, and lightning flashed.

The little girl was snatched back into the painting too. But not before she said, "Goodbye, Carrie. My spirit is free now because you dared to care about me. This is all but a painting now. I love you, Carrie."

Phoenix relaxed. He looked at the children with big hazel eyes. Jason said to Carl, "What did you do?"

"It's simple, when you fight a demon king, there's always something that will defeat him. You just have to find out what it is and take it. It's like finding a magic crown and winning the game. The bonnet was like the crown that held the little girl. It was on her head, so rather than put it on an avatar's head, I had to take it off her head. That flowered bonnet made her suffer. I don't know about those two guys and what they did, but I know the bonnet was just like a 'crown of suffering' or something. That little girl was suffering because of those two guys. She wasn't bad. It was the bonnet on her head that held the key. She didn't want to hurt Carrie. The little girl from the painting really wanted to play with Carrie. And the two men were making that little girl suffer. Well, not anymore. Look at the little girl. She's back in the painting. Her hair hangs down in curls, and she looks happy. But how do we explain all this to Mom and Dad?"

"I will!" Carrie said.

Jason said to Carl, "I guess you are the video-game-kid. End Game!"

The Good People

By Stephen Lang

Saturday, 30th March 1901

I hardly touched any supper tonight. I was so excited I could not settle, and I let the candle burn almost to the end before finally opening this journal to write. But where to begin? There is so much to get down as I now have a legitimate occupation as a census taker. It will be good to count the living for a change.

Eliza despairs of me. She says I should find something with better prospects. But it is a start, and Eliza does not know about my former apprenticeship as an enumerator of dead souls.

I am one of fifty thousand census takers in the United Kingdom. I received a fee of one guinea up front, with an extra payment due of three shillings and sixpence for every one hundred counted above the first four hundred. My responsibility may total as many as fifteen hundred people.

But Eliza has already had enough of my facts and figures. She tries to change the subject, but I can think of little else to talk about.

My instructions are as simple as they are reassuring.

To record persons returned as living at midnight on Sunday, March 31st.

Eliza scoffed at the whole enterprise before retiring to bed, saying she could not see the point of gathering such records. She calls it useless information that will be locked away in the vaults for a century, only to see daylight when we are all dead and buried.

It is now after midnight. Like Eliza, London is sleeping. The district of Stratford looks at peace from the window of our attic rooms. I find beauty in the city's calm, but I am not inclined to write about the empty streets. My mind focuses only on tomorrow.

Sunday, 31st March 1901

Eliza made me a packed lunch from last night's leftovers. She straightened my collar, kissed me and wished me luck. It was all very comforting, and I think deep down, she understands the importance of my task. Eliza is, after all, my one true love.

I passed families attending church as I headed towards Plaistow, and in my enthusiasm, I realised I had ventured out too soon and good people would not be in their homes early on a Sunday. My map took me across West Ham Park, and I found a bench to sit and eat my bread and meat, kicking the pigeons away as they scrambled for my crumbs.

I was to leave a schedule at every house or tenement in the district and assure householders the returns would be confidential and not be used to satisfy curiosity. I have rehearsed the line to perfection, like an actor ready to step onstage.

I arrived at Brooks Road in E13, a backstreet marking the edge of my allocated territory. A particular house—number 41—caught my eye as the front door was open. A man stood outside filling a pipe.

"Good morning," I said. "My name is Patrick Keenan. I-"

He addressed me before I could finish. His discoloured teeth hung crooked in shades of brown, indicating illness or neglect.

"James Sinclair," he said. His hand was deadly cold when I shook it, like he'd plunged it into an ice bucket. "Please come in."

The dwelling had two rooms and a scullery, with a stairway leading to a bedroom above. The light was poor, but I could spot the telltale signs of undernourishment from the inhabitants who loitered in the gloom. Sallow skin. Inattentiveness. A baby moaned softly rather than bawling its lungs out. A boy with filthy bare feet sat on the stone floor next to the baby's crib, playing idly with a spinning top.

"The returns will be confidential and not be used to satisfy curiosity," I said as I handed Sinclair the schedule. I wondered if he would have enough time to complete it as so many were in the house. At least a dozen sorry people were in attendance, aged between a few months and forty years.

The wood on the stairway groaned with the weight of a man coming down from the bedroom. He wore a grey vest, and his braces hung loose from his breeches. He pushed past me in his haste to reach safer ground.

"Excuse me," I said.

"Do not mind Mr. Smith," said Sinclair.

The man he'd called Smith turned to leer at me. His bloodshot eyes suggested he had not long risen from a heavy night, although I could not smell alcohol on him. Smith reeked of something more coppery in substance.

"Nathaniel is my brother-in-law," said Sinclair, as if he was required to qualify Smith's sudden entrance to proceedings. "He is just passing through."

The inhabitants of 41 Brooks Road loitered in the shadowy corners. I wondered if they ever had the luxury of leaving this hovel to pass through anywhere else. I turned to Sinclair.

"Are you good people?" I asked.

"Good?" asked Smith, pushing in front of Sinclair to confront me. "What on earth do you mean by that?" He was so close I could see the spidery veins in his eyes.

"Nothing," I said. "Nothing at all. I will call for the completed schedule tomorrow. Good day to you."

Monday, 1st April 1901

I pondered over one too many ales last night. I needed time to think about all the Plaistow dwellings I had visited. I had never considered or cared who lived in such places and what went on inside them until now. Fifteen hundred faces had passed before my eyes in a day. Most of them, I believe, were good people.

But the tavern proved no refuge for me to gather my thoughts A group of journeymen crowded around a piano to sing a tuneless ditty at the top of their voices. Perhaps they were happy because census day was over. If so, I failed to understand their merriment. They'd had one opportunity in their brief lives to be remembered and returned as living. As Eliza had said, it was all useless information that would be locked away in the vaults for a century, only to see daylight when we were all dead and buried. And the journeymen quaffed their ale and sang like there was no tomorrow.

I had nothing to sing about. Nathaniel Smith concerned me too much. I had seen an all too familiar evil behind those red-rimmed eyes.

It was odd I had found only 41 Brooks Road infected in all the places I visited. But I had seen the bloodlust localised before. Once it takes hold, it creeps unnoticed like dry rot under the floorboards. It may not spread far, but the consequences are always devastating. But I soon doubted myself, fearing that the beer only fuelled my fancy. What proper evidence did I have? Taking an instant dislike to somebody was not enough.

Eliza was tearful when I returned. She said census taking would only bring ill tidings if it turned me back to drink so easily. My supper had gone cold, and I left it on the plate untouched. I asked Eliza if she thought me a good person. She did not reply.

I set out early in the morning to collect the schedules. Eliza provided me with fewer leftovers for my packed lunch. I suspected she was already tired of the novelty of making it. Or it was more a case of diminishing returns. The less I ate for supper, the less she would cook the next time. But I had little time to eat, grabbing snatches of my food between the houses I visited. Everyone was at home, ready to surrender their returns to me.

I delayed the inevitable and made Brooks Road my last call of the day. The door to number 41 was again open, and Nathaniel Smith stood outside. His face looked fuller, and his eyes were now clear and bright, although I could still detect the coppery smell, which was now more pungent. His wide-lapelled black suit was of a cut I had seen at funerals.

"Good evening," I said. "May I see the head of the household?"

Smith rubbed his chin. "The head, you say? Would that be Sinclair? Well, I am afraid he is indisposed."

"Indisposed?" I could hardly see beyond Smith's shoulder into the dim interior, making out only the flicker of a shadow on the stairway. A figure descended with light steps that did not cause the wood to creak.

The boy dangled the spinning top from his hand as he took Smith's side at the door. He rubbed his feet against his breeches to clean off the dirt. But the smirk on his greasy face indicated he was not keen to make a good impression, at least not with me.

Smith handed me the schedule. "Is this what you want?"

"Is it completed?"

He smiled to allow me a flash of his teeth, turning away to face the boy before I could fully take them in. But what I saw of the teeth was good. They were pure white. I recognised the sharp canines of a well-nourished monster.

I did not bid them good day in my haste to leave, and they did not acknowledge my departure. Whether I was there did not appear to matter to them. I found a bench in West Ham Park. My satchel was full of paperwork, but I was only interested in one schedule. I clutched it in my hand like a winning ticket.

James Sinclair, aged thirty-nine, listed himself as the head of the household, living with his wife Theresa, aged thirty-five, and nine children, aged between one and fourteen. Nathaniel Smith's name was missing.

Sinclair had added a footnote.

Nathaniel and the boy were passing through. But I had not included them because they are not living. I swear to God that this is true. NATHANIEL AND THE BOY ARE NOT LIVING.

Tuesday, 2nd April 1901

Eliza made an excellent supper last night. We talked of cheerier subjects than census taking. She has many plans for us, and Eliza is sure I will find a good job with prospects. I kept a brave face throughout the conversation and nodded appropriately when she looked at me. She thinks it is all over.

It does not escape me that yesterday was April Fool's Day. I find it an odd choice for a census day. Odd, ironic or perhaps an ill portent. There is a fine of five pounds for giving false information, although the data I have collected from 41 Brooks Road is technically accurate.

My instruction now haunts me. To record persons returned as living at midnight on Sunday, March 31st. I fear Sinclair and the other unfortunate souls at 41 Brooks Road may have joined Smith and the boy as not living.

I have failed to act. I have refused to accept the telltale signs of the stink of Smith and the boy's evil intention. The coppery reek was the smell of blood. Why did I not act?

I gathered together the essential tools required to destroy these foul creatures. I knew I faced a challenge in the limited time, and my detailed notes on vampirism are gone forever. I was foolish to burn my old journals.

Vampirism. It has taken me until now to write the word.

My satchel was almost too heavy to haul across West Ham Park. I dragged it rather than carried it most of the way, but the weight reassured me I was well-equipped.

Nobody stood outside the open door of 41 Brooks Road to greet me. I entered the house and lined the floors of the empty rooms with crucifixes. I climbed the rickety stairs, sprinkled the wood with holy water, and waited in the bedroom, hammer and stake in hand, ready to strike. A filthy linen curtain swayed in the breeze. It was hard to tell if they had escaped this way and taken flight through the window, but I knew they had gone. I did not curse them. I said a prayer instead.

Wednesday, 3rd April 1901

I must copy all the details from the schedules into an enumeration book and deliver it to the local registrar. They will check my work and pass the book to their superintendent to forward to the Census Office in Millbank. The clerks will classify the entries before the issue of the final volume of statistics. I have removed Sinclair's disturbing footnote.

My census takings will pass through many hands. And for what? What will people gather from this a century from now?

I took this journal out with me today. I feared Eliza would read it if I left it at home. I had no packed lunch but felt too sick to eat, my stomach in knots. I sat in West Ham Park to write until the light faded before returning to Stratford.

I walked lifelessly, dawdling because I dreaded what I would find. And my worst fears came true. I found them crowded in each of the lower dwellings of the house. I recognised our fellow tenants and also the trespassers who had joined them. The infected filled every nook and cranny, and I knew they must have followed me to find out where I lived.

The front door was open. I tripped over the spinning top at the bottom of the stairs.

I ran to our attic rooms, taking three stairs at a time. Eliza lay in our bed with the blankets pulled up to her chin. She shivered with a fever, strands of wet hair plastered to her forehead.

The boy sat at the end of the bed. He had drawn up his feet, dirtying the sheets. I pulled the filthy wretch to the floor and cursed him. He looked up at me. There was a tear in his eye—almost human. Then he scuttled away like a spider.

"Eliza? What has happened?"

"Dying," she said. "Dying of the cold."

"Cold? Then I shall shut the window."

I fumbled with the latch before realising that the window was not open.

"She is not bothered by the cold. Eliza is merely a little drained."

It took me a moment to place the voice of the man standing in the dark corner of the room. James Sinclair's face was as bloodless as a statue. I had not seen a walking corpse in years. If he took my hand, I feared the cold would fuse me to him this time.

And there were so many corpses to choose from. All the residents of 41 Brooks Road slowly pushed their way into the room. Sinclair's children were now wide-eyed and attentive. His wife rocked the cooing baby in her arms. I knew their teeth would be whitening. Sharpening.

"Eliza," I said. "Please listen to me. There is not much time. Have I ever spoken to you about vampires?" She shook her head and closed her eyes. "No, I don't recall doing so, but perhaps you have heard me utter something in my sleep? Have you?"

I rubbed Eliza's hands. There was still warmth in them. Deep down, there still was.

"Yes, Patrick," she whispered. "I have often heard you speak of monsters in your sleep. Always at dawn and with a sigh of relief that the threat has passed for another day."

"I am sorry," I said. "Sorry that I could never shake off this terrible calling. That's why I took the role of census taker. I secretly hoped to root out at least one last vampire in London's slums."

"Has it?" she asked. "Has it passed?"

I waited for Smith to come back. There was still a little left of Eliza's blood to drain, you see. I clutched the wooden stake in my left pocket and the hammer in my right.

"No, Eliza," I said. "No, it has not."

Appendix from the Superintendent Registrar

Patrick Keenan entrusted me with his journal on Friday, the fifth of April. He stressed it must not be read for one hundred years so as not to satisfy curiosity, claiming it would provide a valuable footnote to the 1901 census. I have concluded his final wish is not one of a sound mind.

Some would say the man was drunk. I could not tell if it was drink or some other demon that tempered him. He spoke incoherently, praising the safety of a Stratford tavern where he would write. He told me the singing of the journeymen who drank there comforted him, although he refrained from joining in. He called them good people.

Keenan forbade my reading the last page of his journal. He told me all I needed to know was that he had destroyed a monster. Nathaniel Smith had dared him to try, and the others—the other "vampires", as Keenan described them—goaded him on. They wanted a fight. They provoked Keenan into attacking Smith. So he did, placing his hands around Smith's cold throat. A brief struggle followed, Smith overcoming Keenan to pin him to the ground. The stink of blood on Smith's breath almost overcame him, but Keenan summoned enough strength to drive the stake upwards through the monster's heart. Keenan heard the sound of weeping after Smith turned to dust. He swore it came from the bed, from Eliza.

But Keenan was far from satisfied with ridding the world of Nathaniel Smith. He knew he could not destroy babies and children. Or their doting parents. He could not do that. Keenan let them go free to spread the rot further. He had scored one point for humanity but lost many others.

He could not destroy Eliza, his one true love.

Keenan was seen for the last time on Westminster Bridge on the evening of Sunday, the sixteenth of June. The eyewitness I interviewed remains adamant she did not see him jump to his death. It was more that he turned away from her and evaporated into the night like a tired final breath. I find this account hard to believe. But Keenan cannot be traced.

The Handprint

By Megan Russ

A bloody handprint? That was it?

I looked around the alley for other clues. Had there been any from the night before, they were probably currently being washed away by the storm. The man behind me held an umbrella politely over my head as I crouched in the puddles, around bags of trash, and between gutters.

I rubbed at my temples and removed my glasses to wipe the droplets of rain from the lenses. Was a bloody handprint even a crime scene? And what had prompted them to call me?

"Tom, why am I here?" I asked again. The first time I had asked as I crossed under the yellow tape that blocked off the alley I had been shown the handprint.

"The cap thought this would be right up your alley," he said. He grinned at his own joke. I just rolled my eyes and sighed.

"I don't see how this is a crime scene, and how it came under your purview?" I asked. Detective Thomas Berkly, lead investigator of the PEPS. Paranormal Extraordinary Police Squad. PEPS, pronounced 'peeps' by those throughout the civilian community.

"Look Aims, I have no idea, the captain thinks this is something to do with the new gang around the corner," he whispered. He glanced at Captain Liza Perselly on the other side of the yellow tape. She was busy corralling the journalists.

The new gang around the corner was a pack of werewolves. They had moved in a few weeks back. They all had their current permits, and the social worker in charge of their case had already paid them multiple visits to ensure that they were abiding by the law.

"Does this look like a Were attack to you?" I growled.

"No, but..." He was cut off as Captain Liza stepped up to us.

"Mia, did you find anything?"

"No, Captain," I said, "I'm not even sure if this is a crime scene. A bloody handprint isn't much to go on."

"Even with your gifts?" she demanded.

That is all I was to her — a psychic, throwing my god given gift around like a child with glitter. I chewed on the inside of my left cheek for a moment, trying to come up with a polite way of telling her off.

"I just got here. I haven't had the time to yet," I said, "and usually I need something physical to use as a focus. All we have is the handprint."

"Then touch it," she snapped, too much pressure from the press.

"Wouldn't that be tampering with evidence?" I retorted.

"We have our pictures, forensics has samples. You wouldn't be doing anything that this rain isn't already doing for you." She spun on her heel and went back to the crowd of journalists.

I sighed and stepped out from under Thomas's umbrella. I could hear the cameras clicking not twenty feet away as I went to the handprint and put my hand over the blood. With no glove, no protection from any potential contaminant, it had to be physical contact. Please, god, don't let it be vamp blood, I prayed as my hand touched the damp brick. Click, click, the cameras continued, each photographer scrambling to get a picture of the PEPS psychic Mia Cruz.

I reached for the crystal, the amethyst from Australia, that hung around my neck. I closed my eyes as my hand touched the blood, the handprint barely larger than my own. A woman then? I felt the cold envelope me, my skin prickled, and my body went numb.

Images flashed through my mind. Signs that said 'monsters are people too' in big black letters, 'vote yes to #4', then more signs, 'death to monsters', 'vote no to #4', 'hunters for hunting monsters', I shook my head. I saw these images all the time walking into the police station. People held rallies in front of businesses all over the city protesting paranormal legalization issues. It was only one week from the vote on the number four bill to give creatures more rights. Then the image of a man with fangs standing over me, he looked strange, there was no glow to his red eyes, his nose was crooked, his hair greasy, his clothing was new, the collar of his blue shirt flipped up to hide his neck. I could feel the wound in my right arm as he bit me. I felt the scream escape my throat. Then nothing.

"Mia?" Thomas's voice. I opened my eyes. I was still standing in the rain, my hand still on the damp brick. I was shivering. Had I screamed out in pain? It wasn't uncommon for the visions to bleed over into the real world.

"What did you see?" Liza demanded from beside him.

"A vampire." I rubbed my hands through my short hair. I shivered again and looked down at my arm. No mark, fortunately. Sometimes there were bruises.

"Is that your official report?" Liza asked.

"There is more, but I'll need time to get it all out," I growled. Thomas threw a blanket, scratchy, thin, police issue, around my shoulders and walked me away from the press. The other end of the alley was another line of yellow tape, police cars but no press. He opened the door of his sixty-seven Impala and let me fall into the passenger seat.

"What else did you see?" he asked as we drove to the station.

"Protestors for bill four," I said. I stared out the window, the rain dragging along the glass in rivulets as the car sped down the streets, still early enough in the morning that there was barely any traffic.

"Which side?" he asked as we stopped at a light.

"Both," I replied. He looked at me, his green eyes narrowing, a dark eyebrow raised. "I'm as confused as you are."

"So are they dead?"

"Not sure on that one either. The last thing I saw was a vampire biting her arm, but that happens all the time at the freak clubs. A bite doesn't kill someone," I said.

"Maybe they accidentally killed her and they are trying to cover it up," Thomas said.

"It doesn't explain where the body went."

"Maybe the vamps left it in the Were territory, and the Were took it home for a snack?" he asked. I glared at him out of the corner of my eye. He was grinning. He and I both knew that isn't how Weres operate.

"Has the social worker reported anything strange from the pack since it moved in?" I asked.

"Not that I recall, I'll make that priority numero uno when we get to the office just to check," he said happily.

"No, don't bother Shery. We need to look for any missing persons reported in the last twenty-four hours," I said. I pulled out my little black book of notes from my coat pocket and recorded my vision in full. I wrote down everything from the words on the signs to the color of the buttons on the vamp's shirt. I glared at the notes when I was done. Even with everything on the two pages I had written, it wasn't much to go on.

Sure enough, when we got to the precinct there were about fifteen people in front of the building. Even in the rain and the cold, they still wanted us to know they were not happy. This group was against monster citizenship. Their signs were full of hateful words towards those that were less than normal. Unfortunately, I fell into that group. Even as a new member of PEPS, I had already made waves in their group as a psychic. I and all the psychics now on the police payroll were easy targets for their hate.

"Freak!" someone in the crowd yelled at me as Thomas and I climbed from his car.

"Monster!" another roared as we walked around their little protest to get to the double glass doors.

That evening, as I sat glaring at the computer screen on my desk, I mulled over the vision again. The PEPS were contacting every vampire that matched the description of the one in my vision. They would be here thirty minutes after sundown. If they weren't, the hunters would be released on them. It wasn't that vampires were restricted to the night, but the sun hurt them like a horrible sunburn, so it was out of politeness we allowed them to come after sundown.

I closed my eyes, and I could see it all again.

Something was wrong with the vampire. Why were his red eyes so dull? Usually, they would glow in dim light, especially when about to feed. Maybe he was sick, it would help me narrow down the suspects once they arrived. Of course, there was still the problem of no body. Just because this vampire fed on the person who left the handprint doesn't mean they had killed them.

I switched my computer window over to the live stream of a press conference in D.C. The White House press secretary was standing at her podium. Below her, scrolling across the screen was information pertaining to bill number four. In the upper right-hand corner of the screen, the station was playing shots of protests, riots, and even pictures of murdered monsters. My eye was drawn to the images. One image was of a man with three dead Weres at his feet. He stood over them as if they were fifteen-point bucks. The images switched to those supporting the bill. Weres, witches, psychics, humans, a few demons and one angel, locked arms around a group of people protesting the bill, protecting them from their own people. I shook my head and clicked back to my report.

"You would think with the vote so close they would be more careful," Thomas said, breaking me from my staring contest with the screen. I glanced up at him as he leaned against my desk. He handed me a fresh cup of black coffee. We were going to be here for a while. His eyes were on the fifty-five inch flat screen on the other end of the room. It was the same press conference I had on my computer, just from a different news channel, and the images were reversed. The press secretary was in the tiny window on the upper right, and the protestors' images were the large ones on the screen. My stomach rolled as the large image of the man with the dead werewolves in front of him popped up again.

My best friend was a werewolf, and he had never hurt a human in his life. Unless you counted breaking a few hearts with his wolfish grin.

"It's disgusting."

"I agree with you, Aims," he said, using my nickname to put me at ease. He nodded toward the doors as two men walked in. "Looks like we have some company." He rose to his feet and went to greet them.

I recognized them. The one with bloodshot eyes and the wrinkled white shirt was a social worker. I had worked with him on a few cases. He worked mainly with vampires, getting them set up with blood banks, night jobs, and information for freak clubs. The other was a lawyer; a leech was a better term for him. He also represented vampires and was the gopher for one of the oldest vampires in the city. Thomas waved me over to them.

"Look, I'm not saying that they are innocent, but they still need to be treated as fairly as any human," Jeb, the social worker, was telling Thomas.

"We haven't treated them unfairly," Thomas argued.

"If they don't report within thirty minutes of sundown, they are open game," the lawyer Nicolas snapped.

"That is the current law. If this were a few weeks from now, they would have all night to report in," Thomas growled.

"None of my clients would have killed someone," Nicolas retorted.

"You don't represent every vamp in the city," Thomas said, crossing his arms.

"Close enough," I mumbled as I came to stand beside him. "Gentlemen, we are going to take every precaution with this case since it's so close to the vote on number four. Any public outcry now could send it careening into next year."

"You don't even have proof that a crime was committed," Nick snapped.

"By the laws currently in place, a psychic vision is enough to warrant reasonable suspicion," Thomas stated. Nicolas glared at me. He was not convinced, or was it that his clients were not convinced?

An hour later, I was sitting in a dim room on the other side of a one-way piece of glass from a group of six vampires. They all stood glaring at the window. I don't know why we bothered with it. Vampires could see in the infrared spectrum. They could see me, Thomas, Jeb and Nick in the tiny room. I stepped up to the glass as the final suspect stepped into the room. Seven of the registered vampires in the city matched my description. I looked over my shoulder at Thomas and shook my head.

"I don't think it's any of them," I said after a moment.

"I told you," Nicolas snapped.

"I want to take a closer look at them," I growled.

"Do you think that's wise?" Thomas asked.

"Well, they could invoke the sixth amendment and I would have to face them anyway," I said, leaving the room and walking the ten feet to the door, stepping into the room with the seven vampires. They all turned to watch me.

The hair on my neck and down my spine stood on end. Like a rabbit in the sight of a hawk, I could feel the predator's gaze upon me. I stepped in and closed the door behind me. They were all smart enough not to try anything. I went to the closest and looked up at him. Tall, too tall. His red eyes glowed even in the bright fluorescent lighting. He was at least two hundred, far too powerful for me to see him in a vision. I shook my head and told him to go home. I went to the next, and the next, and on until I had looked into the faces of all seven.

"It's a dead end then?" Thomas asked as his lith form leaned against the door frame. The last vampire was grabbing a cup of coffee in the waiting room before he left. Vampires like coffee, even cheap instant coffee that the station had for free.

"Tomorrow, I want to go speak to the alpha of that new pack, see if they know anything," I stated. I went to my desk and got my coat.

"Do you want a ride home?" Thomas asked. He smiled down at me, his green eyes shining with something I could only call hope.

"Not tonight, Tom," I said. I left the precinct and headed to the bus station.

I nodded to the ghoul who was driving the bus as I climbed up the steps. I slid my pass through the reader and took a seat. I pulled my notebook from my pocket and reread my vision again.

"Do you do readings?" a female voice asked. I looked up to see a woman with brown eyes, blond hair, and a weary smile sitting across from me. I sighed. I really needed to start wearing sunglasses, even at night. My purple eyes made it hard to hide in plain sight.

"During office hours, yes," I sighed, closing my notebook.

"Do you have a card?" she asked with another forced smile. I put my hand into my purse, my fingers sliding across my nine millimeter before finding the envelope of cards. I pulled one out and handed it to her.

"I am available from eight until ten in the morning. The rest of the time I am busy," I said. I held out the card. She grabbed my wrist across the alley. Damn it, I had let her get too close.

My eyes rolled up into my head. I screamed and laughed at the same time as I ran from a man with red eyes, but not a vampire, contacts. I watched as he snapped on fake fangs. I led him into the alley. I told him what to do then. He bit my arm, spitting the blood onto my hand, so I could make the handprint on the wall. "All according to plan," I said.

I came to, a man with glowing green eyes shaking me awake—the ghoul, the bus driver. I sat up shaking. I put my hand on my head. "What happened?" I asked, my throat felt raw, like I had just drunk coffee straight from the filter.

"I think you were having a vision," the ghoul said. I nodded. I looked at the seat across from me, empty.

"Where'd she go?" I asked. He looked at the empty seat and shook his head.

"I think she got off when I stopped the bus," he said. I jumped to my feet. Bad idea, I had to grab the railing to steady myself. This is why I preferred reading cards and crystal balls over contact with humans. I went through the open door at the back of the bus and jumped to the sidewalk. The few people walking down the street glanced at me, then away. They saw my eyes just as she had, a freak. I climbed back onto the bus and sat back down, near the driver.

"Do you know who she is?" I asked, leaning my head against the cool glass as the bus rumbled forward.

"Never seen her before."

Great, I thought. I found our victim, but she got away.

I pulled my phone from my back pocket and called Thomas. With no answer, I left a message about what had just happened. "Tom, call me. I have a lead. Our victim is alive," I said. I hit the end button as the bus arrived at my stop. I got off, thanking the ghoul. I turned to the right and headed towards my apartment.

The night desk clerk was a vampire, young, only five years turned. He nodded to me as I came through the revolving door. "You're home late."

"I had to interview a few vampires," I sighed.

"Were my brethren at least helpful?" he asked.

"They were cooperative, but the case hit a dead end," I said.

"I saw you on the news when I got up, something about a missing person and a bloody handprint?" he asked. I nodded as I hit the elevator call button. "I find it hard to believe any of us would do anything to jeopardize the vote," he said.

"You'd be surprised. But I hope you're right. Good night," I said as I climbed onto the elevator and hit the number four button.

The next morning I sat at my desk at the consulting firm, Daylighters, twirling an incense stick as I stared at the deck of tarot cards in front of me. Business from human clients was slow with the vote for the new law so close. Most of them didn't want to be seen in a business run by freaks.

"What's on your mind?" Derian asked from where he peeked over the cubicle wall down at me. His glowing orange eyes, his thick beard, and messy black hair, went perfectly with the wolfish grin he shot me as I glanced up at him.

"Bothered by the case I'm working on," I replied with a sigh. He vanished over the cubicle and appeared in my entrance a moment later. He fell into one of the two chairs across from me and picked up the deck from my desk. Without a word, he shuffled and split the deck and handed it back to me. I rolled my eyes and took the cards from him. "What is your question today?" I said in my most exaggerated fortune teller voice.

"Will I ever find love?" he asked, swooning with his hands held under his chin. He batted his eyelashes at me. I couldn't help but grin. I shook my head and pulled the cards from the deck in the right order.

The Ten of Swords, Ace of Pentacles, and the Tower. Derian cocked his head at the cards, as did I. "That can't be good," he whispered. We both jumped as my cell rang. I looked down at the number. It was the precinct.

"No." I put the phone to my ear. "Mia Cruz."

"Mia, have you heard from Thomas?" Liza's voice came over the phone.

"No, not since the office last night, why?"

"He didn't come into work today, and we have another bloody handprint, this time with a body," she said.

"Do we have an ID?" I asked. I grabbed my purse from under my desk and climbed to my feet. I nodded to Darian, he followed me.

"No, we just got the call from the fifth," Liza said. "Dammit, where is that man? I'll meet you there. I'll text you the address." The call ended as I pushed out the fogged glass door with the words 'Daylighters Consultants' in big gold lettering. Darian was right on my heels.

"I'm coming with you this time," he said as we stepped onto the sidewalk outside the old brick building.

"Good, I might need your nose," I said. We hailed a taxi, and I gave the driver the address.

I climbed out of the cab as Darian paid and was stopped by Liza. Her face was white, hands shaking as she held me by the shoulder. Darian stepped out from behind me. I heard him take a deep breath. He let it out in a rush. I turned to look at him. His orange eyes were wide.

"Captain?" I asked, trying to push past her. I could see the yellow tape and a tarp covering the body. The tarp didn't quite cover the tall man beneath. The old worn combat boots with the neon green laces were exposed at one end. I fell to my knees, my mouth open. I shook my head.

"I think you need to go home," Liza said, looking at Darian, "take her home."

"No," I said, climbing back to my feet and shoving past the captain and under the yellow tape. The press was starting to arrive. I went to his body and kneeled beside the tarp. I pulled it back. Tears flowed from my eyes as I stared down at his face. They hadn't closed his eyes when they covered him. He stared up at the sky, his mouth open, his eyes wide. He had died in fear.

"Mia don't," Darian said from behind me as I reached out and touched his cheek.

I was walking through the parking garage of my building. My hand went to my gun when I heard footsteps behind me. I spun to see a man with dull red eyes. He reached toward me. I dodged back and pulled my gun. I got off one shot before something hit me from behind. I opened my eyes again. I was in the back of a van, my hands tied behind my back. I fought against the ropes and bit at the gag in my mouth. Two women sat in the back of the van with me, one with brown eyes and blond hair, the other a redhead, both human. The man with the dull red eyes was driving the van.

"He's awake," the redhead said.

"Good, we are about there," the man said. The van stopped, and I watched him slip on the fake fangs. I was dragged from the van and dropped onto the wet concrete of an alley.

"Any last words?" the man asked, getting really close to my face, making sure I saw his red eyes and his fangs.

"They aren't real Aims," I whispered as the gag was removed. The needle slid into my neck, and everything went dark.

I opened my eyes, tears streaming down my cheeks. Darian was holding me, and when he saw the color return to my eyes, he picked me up and took me to a waiting police car. My hand trembled as I wrote the vision in my book. My vision blurred as tears kept filling my eyes with every blink. Darian's warm arm around my shoulders kept me grounded as the police car carried us to the station.

I don't remember walking into the building or even walking to my desk. I don't remember who put the coffee in my hands. I do remember the chief's foot tapping incessantly beside my desk. I looked up at the rotund old man as he glared down at me.

"Well psychic, who killed our boy?" he demanded.

"Humans," I whispered. He huffed.

"No, there are vamp marks on his neck," he snapped.

I shook my head. "Fake, it's fake, they poisoned him," I argued. My voice sounded far away. I jumped as a hand landed on my shoulder. My shoulders relaxed as I looked up into Darian's orange eyes. His presence gave me a little more comfort.

"Why would humans do this?" he roared. Waving his thick arms, he looked like one of those wiggly advertising things in front of a used car dealer. His face was almost as red.

"The new law," Darian stated flatly. The chief glared at him.

"I didn't ask you, mutt," Chief Gonzalez spat. I felt Darian's hand on my shoulder tighten. I reached up and placed my hand on top of his. "Why are you even here? Didn't we fire you?" he demanded.

"You did, but I'm here for my friend," Darian replied.

"He's right chief, with the vote so close, any uproar now might delay it or cause it to fail altogether," I replied. "It wouldn't be the first time extremists would go to such lengths," I added. "Send the artist here. I can give a description of all three of them." My voice was a little steadier. The chief glared at me, but nodded. He stomped away and waved for the sketch artist to go to me.

"If I had let him drive me home, he would still be here," I said. Darian cocked his head, his orange eyes narrowed.

"Mia, don't say things like that. It's not your fault," he stated. I shook my head. He kneeled to wrap me in a tight hug, rocking me back and forth. "It's not your fault," he whispered in my ear.

It didn't take long for the press to catch wind of the story. It was quickly spun into a conspiracy theory all over the web. The screen in the bullpen was turned up so everyone could hear as we watched Captain Liza on the screen.

"We have suspects, and we are not at liberty to release any new information at this time. We do know that this is related to the new bill in Washington regarding further freedoms regarding our supernatural friends," she said. We could have been there beside her listening as she said it. She was only fifty feet away, outside the glass doors to the station. "Our belief is that a group of pro-human activists are to blame, but we cannot confirm that at this time."

Three hours later, the suspects were marched through the doors, all in handcuffs. The man was still wearing his fake vampire contacts and teeth. The redhead was sobbing uncontrollably, professing her innocence to the world as she was dragged through the glass doors. A line of police kept the press back, but it didn't prevent them from snapping pictures of the suspects. The blonde glared at me with a smirk on her face as she was pulled through the hall. The man was growling and raging at the two officers who held him. As if his ruse was still working, if he was a real vampire, the steel cuffs he was in would be doing nothing but decorating his wrists. The PEPS officers were not fooled by the man's act, and he was thrown into the interrogation room and cuffed to the table just as any human. No need to call the werewolf guards to make sure he kept quiet. The women confessed first, and with their words against him, the fake vampire soon folded as well.

Another hour and the captain was back in front of the cameras with the police's official report. "Three suspects are in custody. They used false contacts and teeth to try to pass as vampires. They are now being connected to three other murders around the city. These people acted alone, but are affiliated with the Humans for Humans, Death to Monsters, and Hunters for Legal Game associations. These groups have denied any involvement, but it is believed that these three acted in order to prevent number four from passing in the House next week." I turned away from the screen as she asked the press if they had any questions.

"You look like you could use a drink," Darian said from the edge of my desk.

One week later, number four passed in the House with an amazing four hundred votes for. Three weeks later, the bill passed in the Senate.

The partners of the Daylighters had brought in a large flat-screen television from one of their houses for the day the bill was signed into law three months later. We all stood around our break room eating pizza and drinking soda.

“Hush, it’s happening,” our boss yelled from near the screen. We all turned to watch as the president set her pen down and held up the new law. We cheered and toasted.

“To Thomas,” I said to Darian. He hit his can of diet cola against mine, and we drank to Thomas, who had died for the sake of the new law.

The Hands of Others

By J. G. Davies-McCabe

It was early October when the house came up for sale. Of course, I viewed it in its entirety even though I knew the layout well and all of its intricacies like the back of my hand. I knew where the walls warped, the ceiling drooped, and the shadows darkened.

You see, in years long since passed, perhaps fifteen now as I am well into my forties and took up here in my twenties, I had worked here. It had been a "workhouse" not in the traditional sense but in the literal sense. It had been a rather well-reputed home for "challenged children". Somewhat like a care home, but the kind that social services might provide for children taken into its care.

But of course, it had become privately owned and funded and was housing children referred by the parents who struggled to deal with them on a day by day basis, be that because of general behavior or what the daily undertakings of said disability entailed. The hours were long, and the work was hard, but overall it had been good, rewarding work.

I left the service in my mid-twenties and a few months later the home shut down. There was an incident, and the authorities had swarmed the place and kept it locked up tight.

The "incident" in question was, as with most cases involving children, especially those of a disabled disposition, hushed up. No blame was ever found, but in return for silence on the matter, the home was closed.

For years after I bummed around from job to job, vocation to vocation. But now I found myself oddly drawn to the overgrown garden and drooping eaves of the strange house I once spent many an hour inside, filled with laughter, love, and of course, though rather wrongly, fear.

Children are naturally fearful. This is well known, but no one is more so fearful than the parents are. Especially when their beloved and ultimately vulnerable offspring are placed with care into the hands of others, expecting almost unreasonably a level of love and devotion that comes only from the birth of your own child.

I had walked that path in life with a partner who had long since become estranged from me. She had become very ill eight months into the pregnancy, and the child was lost. The crushing, overwhelming horror of it all warped my views on parenthood, and I grew cold and distant, never attempting or even trying to reconcile and try down that path again. Bitterness had overtaken my soul, my heart, and my being in total.

I had spent the last five or so years in my own company. Lonely though it may be, it provided a level of clearheadedness and clarity that couldn't be found amidst a family setting.

The house paperwork went through in mid October and I was moved in rather swiftly on the twenty fifth. I didn't stay the first night that I officially moved in, instead I booked a hotel to sleep for the night. But I spent the day and the evening unpacking and tracing my steps back through the old house and seeing where it bowed and scraped. My reason for not staying in the house I had purchased was almost nonexistent, other than it truly didn't feel right. Inexplicable perhaps, but I didn't feel comfortable or safe on the portable fishing bed I had brought with me, lit rather poorly by the dim light in the small bedroom I had claimed as my own against the backdrop of the cold winter evenings of the south-west of England.

There were plenty of rooms. Four in total that could have been used as bedrooms and others that were used as a dining room, a kitchen, and of course, a sitting room.

The house was firmly planted back several generations and had clearly not been gutted or replaced in a very long time, perhaps with the exception of a new and shiny gas cooker and stovetop that sat out of place in the kitchen.

There was a small conservatory that had been used in the times I'd spent here in years past. It was a small agricultural plot, full of small flowers and assorted faster growing vegetables to give the children that stayed and the ones that came to visit friends regularly something to maintain and feel satisfaction in as they grew.

Of course, many didn't understand it at all and simply liked the colors and twisting of stems and bold protrusions that we call flowers. The blood reds and sun yellows always attracted the most foot traffic through the conservatory.

A note on flowers, though, and plants: over time they change. They grow twisted and warped, and some even grow or start carnivorous, luring in passersby with pretty colors only to be taken apart with acid or fibrous teeth in the very grips of trust. The house had changed that way too. Growing older and colder and home too many an exquisite and most assuredly horrifying change. The natural world shifts and changes, but so does brick and mortar, and especially that which is contained within its stone tapes, but I digress.

My gardening experience was a long time ago, and it was clear no particular gardening expertise had been used in quite some time, as it had simply become a cold outdoor storage room.

A shame, but as time passed, I planned to renovate and start anew. Taking bits and pieces from my past, from the life I had lived a long time ago, and using them to give me pleasure in my current place in life. Bits and pieces, only ever bits and pieces.

The night at the hotel was fine. As standardized and cookie-cutter as you could expect from a chain hotel, and in all honesty, it only took away from the deceitful majesty of the house I was going back to. The one I had stupidly bought, the one that, despite my best thoughts to the contrary, terrified me. The thought of its arches and single-glazed windows icing up in winter sent a cold shiver down my spine. But still, I bought the thing. For old time's sake.

I unlocked the sturdy old door and went into the dining room. I still had very much left to unpack, but a level of anticipation was vibrating through my very being, like an electric shock across sodden skin, and I yearned to disperse it out through the house.

I rose and padded into the kitchen, pulling my jacket tighter around myself almost unconsciously. I felt cold, and I felt unsure. At this point, I wondered why I had bought this place. Why on earth would you buy a house that unsettled you and horrified you more and more with every step? We'll find the truth lies in memories. In actions and emotions long since past.

You can't ever reclaim the past, experience it again, or anything of the sort, but you can for all intents and purposes immerse yourself in it. And in the end you will either leave beaming with nostalgia, or sick to the very stomach with shadows you had long forgotten still lurked, grey haired and raving mad.

I went up the old uncarpeted stairs, stained with a single rough line of paint off to the left-hand side, and arrived on the five-way landing upstairs. Then there was a choice between four bedrooms and a bathroom.

The bathroom was a yellowed, rough-looking thing. It seemed more like it had been smoke-stained after years of heavy smoking, but was indeed this color by choice. A definite and confusing relic of another age.

I looked through each room in turn, except the one I'd chosen as my own, and found there to be little of interest. Several of the windows were still single glazed and rather thin and the one window that faced out toward the road was home to a rather nasty crack. It was like something else wanted to dismantle the house, so it had started on the softest, weakest part.

Of course, this room was cold, but my insides made it colder. This had been *his* room, the boy of whom the "incident" concerned. Robert Walton was his name, and he was six at the time of its happening.

I remember him being up here. I remember the stamping and the screaming. The unfocused eyes and shaking hands. I fled from the room as the memories piled in.

Perhaps I deserved this? The horror that came with memories, in fact, in a strange way, it was what I hoped for. An understanding, or maybe even vindication, for myself through torment.

All I was doing at this point was tormenting myself. A tear welled in my eyes as I went downstairs and sat back in the dining room. I turned on the old boiler and waited the half hour or so it took for the heat to seep into the icy room. But honestly, it did very little to dispel the coldness I felt.

The day left, and night came, crawling as it always does, and I spent much of it immersed in thought and in memories. I decided to retire for the night; I've never felt smaller than I did on that fishing bed in an empty room beside the single cheap plywood closet. Like a child. Like he who had occupied this place in the past. Except my dwelling was that which came with adulthood, necessity.

The children had decorated their rooms and filled them with loving odds and ends. They may have not been fully sound of mind, but they were definitely pure of heart. I studied the walls in the darkness and thought I espied a peeling and sun-bleached dinosaur sticker tattooed low on the wall along the skirting board. I kept my eyes on it until I drifted off. I slept, but what I did have was restless.

I awoke and checked the alarm clock I'd set up beside the fishing bed, and it was just after three in the morning. I thought perhaps due to my trepidation I'd awoken purely based on nerves and my unceasingly restless mind, but as I began to attune to the darkness and the very small palate of sounds, I realized quite quickly why I had awoken.

Sounds in the darkness, and it was an unmistakable sound—that of scuffed feet dragging along the wooden floorboards. Like a small body was running in the dark with its body hunched over and it hadn't picked up its feet. That or the sound of a small body being pulled across flooring.

I bolted upright and for a second was sure my heart had stopped pumping in my chest. The sounds died down, and I almost laughed at my own stupidity. The noises had stopped by the closet, which was right next to a small ventilation unit. I don't know why I hadn't considered that; it was an old house, of course there were rats in the walls.

I laughed in the darkness, barely seeing the walls and closet made out in the pale milky moonlight. Something crashed against the inside of the closet and rocked it to the side.

I launched further upwards in bed, pulling my duvet with me up around my ears in the most primitive, childlike manner, whilst a cold sweat began to work its way down my forehead.

Strangely, that did little to alleviate my terror. For it was the footsteps that followed that only made my pulse increase and the hackles on my back stand. I'd never felt such pure terror.

It was then that I noticed the lightness of the footfalls. Almost as if...

The footsteps stopped, and in my unthinking state I threw off the duvet and looked around the room. I don't know what I expected, but I was met with nothing but darkness. Darkness, and a sense of guilt.

I scanned the room and realized I had left the door just somewhat ajar, and for a second—a mere fraction—I was sure I saw what looked like part of a small foot shod in a child's shoe leave through the doorway.

I was sure for a moment that my heart stopped, and truthfully in some horrifying way I wished it had, as only one word could describe my situation besides fearful. And that was, of course, guilt. Again, that word, like déjà vu, returned again and again, and I suppose if I am to gain any rest, vindication, or whatever I wish to call it, I should offer some level of honesty and clarity.

I had worked at the house for a few months when Robert took up residence. He had been assigned a room as his parents wished him to stay a few nights a week. I took an instant, and almost unreasonable, dislike to the boy. Of course, back In the day he was just considered a “problem” child or simply "naughty", but in the modern day would probably be labelled as autistic, or at the very least developmentally delayed.

He was prone to violence, often closing his eyes, screeching like a banshee and throwing his fists, his feet, and biting. I should have had more patience, more understanding of the small and vulnerable child. I should have.

And this was why the closet upset me so, rather selfishly perhaps, but the horror it sent through me was almost entirely created of guilt. For on one occasion the boy had lashed out, spitting and biting in his room, whilst I was trying to restrain him whilst he was having a seizure. Something happened, and his small, delicate fist collided with my nose. A rage flew through me, and I grasped the boy, still seizing, and flung him face first into the cupboard. Quickly realizing the sheer audacity and evil of my actions, I shut the doors, locked them, and continued to hold the doors shut as the boy rocked and shook.

It was during his seizure that I grew cold and callous, thinking not of his welfare but of my own. “How could I justify this? What would I say if he spoke out?” But, it was at that moment I knew that the age-old adage of man having both good and evil became true for me, as the most disturbing point stood out in my mind.

“If I got away with this, what *else* was possible?” The thought horrified me, but if I were to pretend that it wasn’t a thought I'd be lying.

When I opened the closet doors, he was still seizing, but only lightly, and hadn’t quite come out of the “trance” that befell him. It took a minute or two, but he finally came out of it. A thick coating of blood over his small innocent face, caused by him hitting the backboard of the closet with such a force, led him to scream upon emerging.

And I too joined in. "Help! Help! Roberts had an accident!" Clearly the poor bastard couldn't remember anything, as the moment he came out of it he flung his meagre arms around me and cried, sobbing deeply, hurt.

"Help, please, me," he said.

"It's okay, it's okay, Robert. I'm here." I set my arms around him too. And squeezed a little too tight.

Yes, I realize the light this paints me in at this point. Honestly, I care very little. For the truth of my purchase was vastly simpler than the lies I've concocted so far. The truth is I wanted some kind of vindication, some kind of forgiveness. And failing that? Well, I'm old enough and have achieved very little. I shall take the coward's way out and open my wrists in this old cold house. For you, Robert, or for me at the very least. The lines blur; I care very little.

The next few days passed with little in the way of incident, unless you count my wearing mental state to be of any importance. And I'm sure you don't ... because I'm the villain here, aren't I? Perhaps I should end this quicker. Perhaps that's what you want?

Another digression, I apologize. And strange as it grew closer and closer to that fateful day I was surprised the house seemed to grow warmer. The boiler wasn't on, only when necessary. The windows were open at regular intervals to clear out the stuffy air that accumulated. And the actual outside only grew colder as October progressed.

The 31st approached, and I had deemed this a very special day for multiple reasons of which I promise I will divulge, but for now I will start off lightly. I intended to decorate the house.

To be an object of desire for the hopefully legions of children that would stumble by: witches and wizards and skeletons and Frankenstein's monsters. I wanted to be THAT house. The one the children all spoke about at school the next day. So, I set about decorating my frontage with scary, yet family-friendly horrors.

Smiling bulbous spiders on bright red webs, cackling witch danglers above cauldrons on strings, and bloody handprints on the windows, just to name a few.

I also bought several tubs worth of sweets and filled a rather large plastic jack-o'-lantern with said sweets and intended to hand them out on the fateful Samhain eve.

Perhaps I should explain why, and I will, but for now my idea was this: if I could get the adoration of the children, perhaps even the respect of some them on this night when the gates were weakest and the dead walked the earth in flesh suits and other assorted ethereal horrors, then perhaps I could receive some kind of forgiveness from the child whom I had wronged.

The days passed slowly, and very little happened. In fact, besides my horrifying experience by the closet, I would pass it off as dreadfully mundane. I even grew, rather surprisingly, to feel a sense of security. But I knew this could only be short-lived, couldn't it?

The day came not with a bang, as the Americans have portrayed in almost all Halloween-themed media, but with a whimper. Almost nowhere bore decorations, and it took nearly all day for spooks and skeletons to make themselves known.

The evening wore on, and the dim yellow light of the streetlights began to highlight that which now roamed the streets: infrequent but no less giddy swarms of young children, infants even sometimes, and of course the occasional "too old for this" types. But I obliged them anyway, filling each bucket to the very rim and being met with ear to ear grins as they ran off.

Now I suppose it is time for the final revelation, and the one I wished not to divulge in any manner but must if I am to receive any level of forgiveness or ... well, anything.

The night Robert died was this night. It was many years ago, Halloween night, and he had died in my care. This may not be a particular shock. Indeed, many an astute reader might have guessed this earlier, BUT the details, to this day, to this very document are not known. They shall be now.

The other two staff on hand that night, I believe Mary and Jonathan may have been their names—not that it matters much—had taken the rest of the children trick-or-treating.

The children, as children generally are on Halloween, were fully decked out in all the appropriate Halloween garb, all except Robert. He wouldn't wear a costume and most definitely wouldn't allow the application of face paint.

I pleaded with him to go, as much for my own sanity as his own hopeful satisfaction, but all was in vain. Instead, he sat in front of the television and watched an old black and white horror film that was being run on channel four.

The boy, as he wouldn't be getting much because of his refusal to go out with the other children, had been given a small bucket of sweets. He sat carefully removing wrappers and eating the sweets one by one.

I once more asked him. "Come on, lad, shall we go out? It's good fun, and you'll get plenty more out there than you will in here!" I tried to inject enthusiasm into my voice, and all I could really muster up was pleading.

My advance was met with screaming, and much to Robert's detriment, the screaming started as a piece of hard candy went into his mouth, flew past his teeth, and lodged itself in the back of his throat. He plunged his hands into his mouth, coughing and clawing, and for a moment I was taken aback. What exactly was happening here?

A second or so later, and perhaps unbelievably, I sprung into action. On my feet and beside the boy, I bent him at the waist and lined my hand upon his back to deliver hasty, yet powerful blows. But as I went to administer the first one, I noticed that the boy's face was turning a shade of bluey grey, and I wish I didn't have to admit this, but I saw an opportunity.

I lowered my hand and set both hands about his shoulders as pleading eyes and a voiceless mouth pleaded silently for help. I grasped him tightly and led his powerless frame to the cupboard that sat below the stairs.

I knew the cupboard was seldom used. Instead, it housed a few loose toilet rolls and a broom. I opened the small door, which held fast with the simplicity of a cheap latch, and bungled the boy with his small weakening frame in through the door.

I'll never forget the look in his eyes as he turned towards the door, the blue on his face bringing out the veins which now stood taut against his skin, and that look in his eyes. Betrayal.

I saw him clawing at his throat once again as the door closed and the latch slid across. Thunderous blows landed in the silence of the house, and the silent voice screamed raspily on the other side, the lodging in his throat keeping the terrible sound in.

He pounded for a minute or so before he fell silent, and I unlatched the door, not even checking as I knew he was dead.

In an almost hypnotic daze, I went back into the front room and set about reading a newspaper. I knew what I'd done, but I knew the biggest part came now, the deception. And when it came, I played it well.

I'd become a snake, a wolf in human skin taking advantage and being callous. But so far? It had only served me well. And the death of the annoying brat was only helpful as far as I was concerned.

Questions were asked, answers were given, but in the end it was ruled that the boy had become locked under the stairs of his own volition, choked on a sweet, and died.

Even though perhaps it was negligent, I was absolved of any wrongdoing and simply let go. This was the scandal that shut the home down. And now I was here to give my penance.

As the night wore on, it was around eight that I handed out my last piece of candy. I said goodbye to the children on my doorstep and turned around a sign that said "No sweets left, sorry!" and went back in to deal with the rest of what may come.

I sat down for ten or so minutes, drank a coffee and thought about whether I could do what needed to be done. If what I wanted couldn't happen, it wouldn't be long until the decision was made for me.

An almost deafening thud crashing against the inside of the door under the stairs nearly threw me from my seat, and it was then I knew that the end was in sight. But why were the thuds so loud? Robert was only a boy, and surely if he had returned, then he had returned as such.

I got into the hallway and looked towards the door in the gloomy light. I saw the door rock under the force of three more heavy blows. Again, with three more the door buckled and bent. Under the force of the final three, as I was rooted in place, the door separated into two halves barely kept together by the cheap latch, which I only now noticed had held after all these years.

Something serpentine slithered out. It seemed to go on forever. I was stuck, like I had taken up roots at this very spot as I watched it come. And come. And continue.

Whatever it was, whatever guise Robert had undertaken, was coated in a layer of thick, lank, and disgustingly matted hair. Whatever the serpentine thing was turned, and I felt the contents of my bladder trickle down my leg and collect in a puddle at my feet as I gazed into eyes I had once known.

They had greyed now in death and I had only a moment to process what I was seeing before the horrible, naked apparition of a fully grown Robert, plastered in bedraggled hair and pale grey skin, crisscrossed with almost luminous blue veins in the darkness. It reached out its terrible hand towards me, the nails of which were at least twenty centimeters long and curled back into themselves, which would've added more than a few inches each.

If it were any other situation, I almost would've laughed at the absurdity of the nails if it hadn't hit me all at once: wherever Robert went after he died, he kept growing.

The naked thing slithered towards me and angled upwards its head, jetting forward in a burst of speed only counteracted by how fast it could slither side to side.

This made rocket backfall over my own feet and into my self-made puddle as the horrible thing stopped mere inches from me and shook.

The fucking apparition was having a seizure. It was almost absurd, and if I didn't think my death was imminent, I'd perhaps have laughed. Instead? I began to cry, screaming and sobbing uncontrollably.

"I am sorry, Robert! Please forgive me for what I've done! You didn't deserve this! Claim me if you wish! But please give me your forgiveness!"

The small TV I had brought with me turned on behind me, and almost on instinct I turned my head backwards and caught what was on the screen. An old black and white horror film, playing on channel four.

Robert's seizure stopped, and the horrible thing slithered with wet, grasping, yet unsure hands, up my body, stopping at my face to stare deeply at me. His mouth opened, and I was sure for a second I was about to become dinner for some beast from beyond, but instead an almost silent, imperceptible scream leapt from its throat. After a few seconds of its silent screams and my very, very audible ones, something launched from Robert's throat.

His screams stopped, and before I could see what it was, he palmed the object in his wet hands and forced his fingers into my mouth, ensuring whatever it was would become lodged in my throat. And as I felt that strange flavor of bile and strawberry mix in my mouth, I knew what it was.

And as he rose to his knees, my coughs started as the piece of hard candy stuck in my throat and he dragged me towards the small cupboard, I laughed, almost uncontrollably, from behind the piece of candy. But of course it was silent, and as my large frame was crushed into place, and my breath halted and my vision turned blurry, I knew this was it.

The darkness became total as the now reappeared doors shut. The latch fell into place, and I began to choke.

The Perfect World Doesn't Need You

By Winona Morris

There were so many people in the park that Keely almost couldn't see the grass between them all. The size of the crowd was unthinkable. In fact, it was illegal. She felt nervous being there at all.

It was a small outdoor music festival. Bands played on different stages on the four sides of the park. She was standing in the middle where their music rioted, a cacophony of sounds. It was louder than anything she had ever heard before. Again, completely illegal.

There was a small manmade pond where she stood. A fountain sprayed up from the center, but she couldn't hear the water over all the other noises.

There was a girl standing in front of this fountain, her blond hair pulled into twin pigtails, each one crisscrossed with rainbow ribbon. She had a bright yellow daisy in her hand and was plucking out its petals.

"He loves me," the girl was saying. "He loves me not." Each sentence came on the pluck of a petal.

Noticing that Keely had moved closer to her, the girl laughed and held the nearly naked daisy out towards her.

"Last one's yours!"

Tentatively, Keely reached out and plucked the petal. She pinched the delicate leaflet up to her face, marveling at the simple beauty. The girl clapped her hands and squealed, "He loves you!"

Suddenly, there was an uproar as several vehicles appeared. They looked like large black boxes on wheels. They drove across the grass instead of taking the road around the park. Clumps of mud and sod flew up from the large black tires as they headed directly towards the gathered crowd.

People on the outer edges, closer to the vans, screamed and surged towards the center of the park. Certain they were about to be run down, Keely instinctively reached out and grabbed the girl's hand, crushing the remaining flower stem between their palms.

The vehicles stopped abruptly, and before their motion had come to a stop completely, people were pouring out of them.

Keely didn't understand how so many humans fit in the vehicles, even as large as they were. It reminded her a little of cartoons where an endless parade of clowns would pour out of a tiny wind-up car. Except these people were as far from clownish as you could get. There were no bright and fun colors, no big shoes, no frizzy hair and bulbous red noses. Each person wore black from head to toe, including tinted black face shields that concealed their faces. Their black clothes held no insignia to show who they might be, and each of them had a rifle strung over their shoulder.

As one, the men unslung those rifles and opened fire on the crowd of people.

Already frightened by the sudden approach of the vehicles, the crowd moved en masse, away from the shooters. Keely and her friend tried to hang on to her friend's hand, but the pushing and shoving crowd separated them.

The sound of gunfire was deafening, nothing like she had ever expected or experienced. Keely wanted to run, but her legs wouldn't move. Fear rooted her to the spot, unable to escape the surrounding carnage.

Bodies dropped all around her.

No, she thought. Not bodies. People. These are people!

As suddenly as the pandemonium had begun, it ended. The silence felt heavy and oppressive. There was no motion, not even from the black-clad triggermen.

Sobbing, Keely looked across the sea of once happy festival goers, now prone on the ground. Not too far away, she noticed the back of a blond head, and pigtails with rainbow ribbon. The petal-less stem of a daisy lay on the ground by unmoving, outstretched fingertips.

Keely tore the VR headset off of her and tossed it. The device skipped like a rock across the smooth expanse of the floor before clattering to a stop against the far wall. She kept her eyes squeezed shut, as if that could stop the images from replaying in her mind on repeat.

She heard the soft musical chime that meant the EduAI had reappeared on the monitor at the front of the room.

"Why did you make me watch that?" she demanded.

"History is a part of the curriculum. The Lumos Park Massacre was a major turning point, helping to guide humanity to a Unified World of Enlightenment. That was today's Histories lesson."

"Nobody needs to see something so horrid. Nobody ever. Not for Histories. Not for any reason!"

"Histories are part of the curriculum," the EduAI repeated.

Keely opened her eyes and turned to look at the screen.

She had never customized her EduAI. The generic female avatar on her screen sat at a desk in a bare room. Her shirt was white, her slacks were khaki, her brown hair pulled back in a severe bun. Behind her thin black glasses, her face was impassive, unbothered by the violent history lesson, unbothered by anything ever.

"It must be nice not to have any feelings." She didn't move to wipe away the tears running down her face.

Another soft chime came from the screen.

"Edu lessons are done for the day, Keely King. We will continue our lessons on the Histories of Pre-Enightened Earth tomorrow."

Instead of fading to black as usual, her Edu screen shifted views.

The image on the screen now wasn't AI. A stern-looking woman sat in a high-backed office chair behind a large black desk. A tablet lay on the desk in front of her, casting a white glow up onto her face.

"Keely King?" she asked.

"Yes, ma'am." Keely swiped the tears off of her face, trying to be discreet but knowing it was too late for discretion.

"Keely King, you have shown strong emotion every day for the past week at this time. Why is that?"

"My Histories lessons," she said. "The VR is very...disturbing."

"Lessons are to impart knowledge. There are no emotions connected to knowledge. Strong emotional responses to immutable events are divergent."

The woman looked down at the tablet in front of her.

"You have displayed elevated heart rates and elevated blood pressure. Your eye motions have registered moments of sadness, of fear and of anger. The markers all indicate signs of hatred, with a high probability of violence."

The woman looked back up towards Keely, her face still rigid but showing no emotion of her own. Keely glanced briefly towards the broken VR helmet on the other side of the room.

"Keely King, it has been decided that you must submit to Transition. You will proceed immediately to Transition Location Lambda, as it is the closest station to your current location. An escort is waiting for you at the front of your home to make sure you arrive safely at the Transition station. Your parents have also been notified."

The screen went blank.

The Lumos Park Massacre, which she had just witnessed firsthand, hadn't been the largest mass murder ever, but it had been the single most pivotal turn in not only her country's history, but the history of the world.

The people's own government had sent those assassins, causing an uproar not only in their citizenship, but in the citizens of every country. The president was overthrown so quickly they didn't even call it a war, and the Unified World of Enlightenment had been born.

It took a few years, but soon the world was really a perfect place.

The utopia was real.

The utopia was temporary.

Perfection came at a price, and that price was Transition.

Keely thought briefly of trying to run, but she knew it was hopeless. Even if she managed to get away from the agent at her front door, which was unlikely, they would still find her. Everyone got a tracking chip at birth. It was a rule.

She knew this was her end. She knew they expected her to go calmly, respectfully, and fulfil her duty.

Eventually, it would be everyone's end. No matter if she had been picked for random Transition, or simply aged out, it always ended the same.

Knowing it didn't matter anymore anyway, Keely screamed. She grabbed her desk and flipped it over. She picked up her stool and threw it at the communication screen, reveling in the way it cracked into a dozen shards. She kept going until she was too exhausted to tip or tear anything else, then finally went out to meet her escort to Transition Location Lambda.

◆◆◆

The building wasn't grand and elaborate. If everyone didn't know what Transition stations were used for, they would have never guessed it. It was small and looked very much like a doctor's office inside. There was a reception desk with a door to the left and another door to the right. Her escort led her to a set of chairs and asked her to sit before going to speak to the man behind the reception desk.

Keely couldn't hear what they were saying, but the receptionist discreetly nodded towards the door, and she turned to see why.

Another escort was coming in, leading her parents.

"Mom!" She couldn't stop herself from crying out. "Daddy!"

They didn't look her way. They didn't even flinch at the sound of her voice. She stood up, but their escort whisked them into the door to the left of the reception desk, and her own escort was looking at her expectantly. She sat back down.

She was still a minor. When a minor was chosen for Transition, their parents had one chance to argue for them. If the argument won, the minor lived, and someone else was chosen.

Her parents were in the unseen room for less than five minutes. When they came out, they didn't have an escort with them, and they exited the building, still never looking her way.

They didn't even try to fight for me, she realized. They went in there and gave them permission. Of course they did. They are young enough to have another child. Why would they fight for one they already know is divergent?

Her top lip curled in disgust, and the mess she left in her room suddenly thrilled her.

"Keely King." Her escort was in front of her. She looked in his face for some sign of sympathy, or even a simple acknowledgement that her parents had not cared about her enough to even argue a little for her. "It has been decided that it is your time for Transition. Please, come with me."

He led her to the room to the right of the reception desk.

Inside, it was also very much like a doctor's office, except for two things. Instead of the usual exam table, there was a hospital stretcher on wheels, covered in a soft cotton sheet instead of a roll of paper. There was also a second door, opposite the one she came in.

When it was over, they would not be taking her back out through the waiting area.

A young woman in blue scrubs stood slightly in front of a small table, which held two vials and two syringes.

Keely's knees went weak, and she thought she might fall, but her escort caught her and helped her to the side of the bed where she sat heavily.

"Keely King," her escort said, "we have notified you of your selection for Transition. Do you know what that means?"

Keely chewed her bottom lip, wondering briefly if she could lie. Those who were not mentally competent enough to know what Transition was were usually spared. They were still removed from society at large, but taken to complexes similar to the orphanages of pre-enlightenment.

She knew better than to try that, however, and just nodded weakly.

"We need you to say it out loud," they prompted.

"When someone is deemed divergent from the rules and expectations of a perfect life as set by the Unified World of Enlightenment they will be Transitioned out of society. It is a humane method in which I will be given a strong sedative, such that I will fall asleep. Once it is determined that I will feel no pain, I will be given a second injection, such that it will stop my heart. The parts of me that can be donated will be harvested, so that despite my divergence, I will still have played my part in the perfect world."

"Very good. Are you going to fight?"

Keely shook her head.

"Good. Now please lie down."

She did as she was told, and the escort left the room, leaving her alone with the young woman.

"You are afraid," the clinician said. "It is natural to be afraid now. You don't have to hide it. Do you want to cry? Many people cry at this point."

Keely shook her head minutely, but her traitorous eyes leaked hot tears down her cheeks anyway.

Keely watched the clinician as she filled the needles. She wasn't really seeing her. Instead of watching her prepare the injection, she pictured her parents turning their backs on her. She pictured the girl from the Histories lesson that morning, plucking petals off the daisy. She envisioned each yellow petal fluttering down until there were none left.

He loves me. He loves me not.

She had been a real person, that girl. She had known true love from her parents, and she had known genuine hatred from those who had mown her down. In between, she had felt unfettered emotion without fearing that those same emotions would be the end of her.

The Unified World of Enlightenment made sure everyone lived in a utopia. Everything always remained clean, harmonious, serene. There was no war, no hunger, no anger. The Unified World of Enlightenment guaranteed civilians a world of peace and love, expecting nothing in return. Nothing except obedience, supplication, and no divergence from what was deemed acceptable.

Could love really even exist in a world where strong emotion is deemed divergent?

First, it is decided that the perfect world doesn't need you, then there is sedation, then there is nothing.

The horror was in how calm it all was. How civilized.

"It's not personal," the technician said, preparing an alcohol swab, as if the prevention of infection mattered at this point, "it's mathematical."

Keely smiled wanly at her.

"I know," she said, and offered her arm.

The Surprise Passenger

By D. L. Garvin

It was Friday afternoon, and I had been looking forward to a long overdue break from work. I was excited to drive home and spend time with family and friends. My job here in Indianapolis is very demanding, and even though home is only three hours away, it's hard for me to get back to Newburgh more than three or four times a year. On this particular trip, I had decided to take I-69, which was shorter than the normal route and newly finished. Things were going well. There was very little traffic, and the weather was perfect—not a cloud in the sky. That was that, until I was about an hour south of Bloomington. The weather changed in a heartbeat. Out of nowhere came a downpour so hard that I had to pull off to the side of the road and wait for the rain to slow down so I could continue.

I didn't have to wait for very long. In about 10 minutes, the rain was down to a drizzle, and I was able to continue my drive. After the rain, the roadway was pretty wet, so I watched my speed. After about 15 minutes, I could see flashing lights and a line of cars stopped, and as I got closer, I could see that there had been a terrible accident between a semi-truck and another vehicle. Both vehicles were off the road and in the ditch. The semi was on its side, and I couldn't tell what the other vehicle was because it was under the truck. I thought to myself, no way that person could have survived.

Since the vehicles were off the road in the ditch, only the right lane was blocked off. There was a deputy sheriff directing traffic over to the left lane, and as I slowly drove past the scene of the accident, I could see all the emergency vehicles. Fire rescue, police, sheriff cars, state police, and two ambulances. And then I saw it. Behind one of the ambulances was a gurney, and on that gurney was a body bag. At that point, my heart sank, and I knew my suspicion was right; at least one person had not survived.

As I drove, my thoughts were on that poor individual who had just lost their life, and wandered about their friends and family. I whispered a short prayer that they would find peace in the afterlife, "whatever that may be." A minute later, I was startled by a movement to my right, and as I turned to look, I was shocked to see a young man sitting in my passenger seat. He then turned and saw me and started freaking out, yelling all sorts of questions about who, where, and why. As I was trying to keep my composure, I slowed down and pulled off to the side of the road. As calmly as I could, I said, "My name is James, and if you calm down, I'll try to help you figure out what is going on."

It took a minute, but finally he started to calm down, and I said first, "What's your name?"

"Michael," he replied, still visibly shaken.

"Okay, Michael, what's the last thing you remember?"

"I was driving home to Evansville from school for the weekend, and it started to rain really hard." He looked at the windshield.

"Well," I twiddled my thumbs, "this may be hard to comprehend, but I just passed a horrible accident on the highway, where I'm sure someone passed away. I think that person may have been you."

Michael sat there for a minute, and I could see tears start to run down his cheek.

"My parents are going to be devastated."

I could hear him choke back a sob. He gave me his address and asked me to tell them that he was sorry and that he loved them. I agreed. Then, there was an air of peace that came over him. He turned and looked to the clouds, and all of a sudden, there was an opening and a bright beam of light streamed down to the car.

"I think that's for you, Michael."

He turned back and smiled. "I think you're right."

He turned back to the light, and I watched as he slowly faded away.

It took a few minutes before I could gather my composure to continue my drive. On the rest of the way home, I played the events over and over again in my mind, trying to make sense of what had just happened. When I finally made it home, it was good to see my family and have a good home-cooked meal at my parents' house. The drive had taken a lot out of me, and I was very tired, but every time I fell asleep, I dreamed about what had happened. The next morning, I slept in, which is not like me. When I finally got up, my father was in the living room watching the local news, and as I walked into the room, I could hear the story. It was about a 21-year-old man who had died in a bad accident on I-69 while driving home from IU in Bloomington, where he was a student. They showed his picture, and it was Michael. It was proof that what happened to me was real and not some crazy hallucination. I was stunned and had to sit down. My father realized something was upsetting me, so he asked, "What's wrong, son?"

I took a deep breath and proceeded to tell him what I had experienced on my way home and the promise I had made. Although he was never a firm believer in the paranormal, he always kept an open mind in such matters. When I was done, he smiled and said, "I think you had an amazing experience, but now you have a promise to keep." I nodded, knowing he was right.

That night, I sat down and composed a letter to Michael's parents, explaining my encounter with their son and the message he asked me to relay to them. The next morning, I dropped the letter in the mail, hoping it would give them at least a little bit of closure.

This was the first and last time something like this ever happened to me, but it is an experience that I will never forget for the rest of my life.

The Tenant

By Ken Austin

The Ouija board was a joke, or at least we thought so.

It appeared at Rachel's Halloween party, stuck between a bowl of candy corn and a skeleton-shaped piñata. "Found it at a garage sale," she said, arching an eyebrow. "Ten bucks says you're too scared to try it."

I rolled my eyes. Sophomores in college didn't believe in ghosts, did they? But tequila shots had blurred the line between stupidity and bravery. Six of us were sitting around the board, fingers on the planchette. "Is anybody here with us?" Rachel asked, giggling.

The planchette jerked to *YES*.

We accused each other of pushing. Then it spelled: *L-I-L-I-T-H*.

"Cut it out," I said, but the room was chilly. The planchette circled the board faster, desperately, until it landed on *GOODBYE*. A bottle of beer was knocked over. We laughed too hard and kept going.

I woke up the next morning with a bruise on my wrist-a perfect circle, black as a burn.

The whispers started on day three.

"Let me in," a voice whispered while I was brushing my teeth. I spat toothpaste into the sink, my heart pounding. My reflection stared back, normal except for the dark circles under my eyes. Had they always been that dark?

By week two, the changes were harder to ignore.

My left pinky finger first locked up. I couldn't flex it. The nail turned gray, then peeled off like old paint. A doctor attributed it to "stress-induced eczema" and prescribed cream. That night, I dreamed of teeth, rows of jagged, yellowed fangs chewing my bones. I awoke to find my sheets drenched in sweat ... and blood. Three parallel gashes marked my forearm, thin as paper cuts.

"You look like hell," my roommate Jess told me, rinsing a coffee mug. Dark strands of my hair clung to the porcelain as she rinsed it.

The voice laughed. "She's right."

The mirror became my enemy.

A rash spread across my collarbone in patchwork scales. The iris of my left eye bleached milky white, and when I blinked, sometimes I'd glimpse her, a creature with too many joints, hunched in the corner of my vision. Lilith.

I studied exorcisms. Burned sage. Recited half-remembered prayers. Nothing worked.

"You need to sleep," Jess said when she found me cleaning the bathroom floor at 3 a.m., the bleach fumes searing my throat. I had not spoken to her about the thing inside me, the thing which whispered "mine" when I touched my rotting skin.

One morning, I couldn't open my jaw. My tongue was puffy, strange. I pried my mouth open with both hands and screamed.

My teeth were sharpening.

By week four, I didn't leave the apartment.

Jess moved out, citing "bad vibes". Can't blame her. The walls oozed black mold when Lilith was upset, and the fridge hummed with flies. I ate takeout with trembling, claw-tipped fingers, weeping as hot sauce dripped down my ripped lips.

"You're almost perfect," Lilith purred.

I tried to cut her out.

The kitchen knife cut unevenly as I slashed at the scales on my chest. Blood, thick and tar-like-bubbled from the cuts. She laughed while I screamed, my cells sewing themselves up again. "Silly girl. We're one flesh now."

The final transformation took place on a night there was no moon.

My back went first, vertebrae popping like fireworks. I flailed on the ground, choking, as my legs twisted into wiry claws. Pain burned through me constantly. Lilith's voice drowned out my screams. "Yes ... YES..."

When she was done, I stood on new legs, my body reshaped by her hands: hard armor covered my ribs, a whipping tail trailed behind me, and my eyes glowed like burning coals. The last shred of "me" cowered in the back of my head, a prisoner in my body.

Lilith stretched my stolen muscles, smiling with my stolen lips.

"Time to play," she purred, and loped into the night.

The news reported it as a "rabid animal attack". Three students were murdered in the campus woods, throats torn out.

I watch the reports from a drainage ditch, my body seething with hunger. Lilith sleeps in the marrow of my bones, satisfied for now.

But soon, she will wake up.

And we'll need to feed again.

Acknowledgement

The Butchered Writers would like to thank every author who trusted us with their work and contributed their voice to this collection. Each story adds its own quiet unease, shaping A Twinge of Terror into what it has become. We also extend our gratitude to the readers who step willingly into the dark — your curiosity is what keeps these stories alive.

About The Author

The Butchered Writers & Contributing Guest Authors

THE BUTCHERED WRITERS:

Andy Holberry, Colt Henderson, D.L. Garvin, Megan Russ, Melinda Pouncey, Raven Tomes & Winona Morris.

~Andy Holberry

Some say he is a failed attempt to merge man and typewriter...those that know him, know the truth.

Andy H is a man of simple pleasures. He lives on a small island just south of the English Channel with his wife, 3 sons, and a tailless cat.

Andy spends every day trying to recreate even a small percentage of what made the British writers of the 80s and 90s some of the best in the world.

His dream is to write that one novel that will give people nightmares.

He has written dozens of stories for anthologies, stand-alone novellas, collaborations, and short story collections, and continues to write for The Butchered Writers; his second family.

~Colt Henderson

Colt M. Henderson lives north of Dallas, Texas with his dog Sir Cottonwood III. He is a prolific writer with an emphasis on horror. He has been published in the Butchered Writers Presents and Terror Monthly series. He is currently working on his first novel about a wendigo.

~D. L. Garvin

Danny Garvin is a retired Cable Television engineer. He's a father of 3 and grandfather of 7 who lives in S/W Indiana in the U.S. and is an avid reader of Science Fiction and all things Paranormal.

He has had a passing interest in writing since high school but started writing more seriously in the past couple of years. His interest in Paranormal stories goes back as far as he can remember, having had a number of paranormal experiences in his life. His blog is a collection of stories that have been told to him over the years by friends and family, as well as stories submitted by readers, and maybe a fictional story or two. He branched out into writing horror in late 2023 when he joined the Butchered Writers, and has contributed over twenty stories to the publication so far.

He has also co-authored the newly released collection Nightmares at the Asylum with his friend and fellow Butchered Writer, Andy Holberry. It can be found at:

https://share.google/RtKeRpWSXCU8Q6JZr

His blog can be found at:

https://paranormalcampfirestories.blogspot.com

The full collection of books by the butchered writers can be found at:

Www.terrormonthly.com

He is active on

X (formerly Twitter) @garvin_danny

Instagram @Danny.garvin.1

TicTok @dlgarvin (DLGARVIN-WRITES)

Blue sky @dlgarvin-writes.bsky.social

Skylight @dlgarvin-writes.bsky.social

~Megan Russ

Megan Russ is the author of the fan favorite Rock Garden, and has been writing with the Butchered Writers since day 1, although her work is not featured in all the volumes due to life circumstances. Diagnosed with Breast Cancer in 2024, right after restarting her self-publishing career, she was forced to step away from horror writing for almost a year until invited back. During that time, she kept sane by playing a homebrew dungeons and dragons game, the game that inspired her new saga, The Miss-Fortunate Adventures. The first book, Lore, is a short story collection that was a finalist in the 2025 BookTok Indie Author Awards. With the success of her short stories, Megan turned to novel writing. Book 1 of the Balance of Fates, Shattered Peace, released in November of 2025 and has been nominated for the SPFBO XI and has been nominated for the Facebook Indie Author Awards. Megan has been writing since 1995 and has no plans to stop any time soon, with the next decade of her writing career laid out in front of her through the Miss-Fortunate Adventures Saga and charity anthologies she participates in by invitation. She will continue to write on and off for the Butchered Writers as themes speak to her. If you liked Rock Garden, just wait for the upcoming Mythology themed anthology.

~Melinda Pouncey

Melinda Pouncey is an author of short stories and flash fiction. She enjoys writing genre fiction, especially horror, mystery, and fantasy. Her stories have appeared in anthologies such as Road Kill 3: Texas Horror by Texas Writers, and Banned by Black Hare Press.

Melinda also writes and edits horror stories with The Butchered Writers, a collective of authors who produce quarterly anthologies based around themes such as urban legends or nightmares. She currently lives in Texas.

~Raven Tomes

Raven Tomes writes horror with a mythic pulse. Stories steeped in mystery, mayhem, and quiet, mournful malice. Her work lingers in the spaces where ancient things stir, where grief sharpens into violence, and where knowledge itself becomes dangerous. The horror is deliberate, patient, and unconcerned with comfort.

Drawn to folklore, curses, obsession, and the unseen mechanisms of power, Raven's stories often feel less written than unearthed. They favor atmosphere over reassurance, inevitability over rescue, and endings that leave a mark rather than an explanation. Someone always knows more. Someone always pays the price.

Under the Raven Tomes name, she explores darker themes and sharper edges—fiction that watches back, remembers its readers, and refuses to look away. This is horror meant to be felt, not softened.

~Winona Morris

Winona always wanted to be a writer when she grew up. When it became apparent that she was never going to grow up, she decided to be a writer anyway. A life-long reader of horror, it turns out she's pretty good at writing it too. Her work leans towards the cozy side of horror, putting character and world building ahead of the shock value. Its not enough to scare her readers, she wants to leave emotional scars. Winona has stories featured in a multitude of horror anthologies, as well as "On Darkened Wings and Other Short Horrors," a collection of her own work.

Winona loves hearing from her fans and would love for you to connect with her on Facebook where she resides as Winona Morris - Author.

CONTRIBUTING GUEST AUTHORS:

Ash Hartwell, Glynn Owen Barrass, J. Rocky Colavito, Ken Austin, JG Davies-McCabe, R.A. King, Sharon Ballentine, Stephen Lang & Thomas Folske.

~Ash Hartwell

Ash Hartwell has a Master's Degree in Creative Writing from Manchester Metropolitan University. His short stories have been published in ezines such as Siren's Call and anthologies from such publishers as Thirteen O'clock Press, Horrified Press, Old Style Press and Nocturn Books. His first novel, Tip of the Iceberg, won best horror novel on Critters(.)org in 2017. His other novel, The Crows of Smith's Booth, didn't. Both are available on Amazon.

~Glynn Owen Barrass

Glynn Owen Barrass lives in the Northeast of England and has been writing since late 2006. He's written over two hundred short stories, novellas, and role-playing game supplements, the majority of which have been published in the UK, the USA, and Japan. To date, he's edited ten anthologies and is part of the editorial team for the magazine Weird Fiction Quarterly.

~J. Rocky Colavito

J. Rocky Colavito is finally an ex-college English professor after thirty plus years on the tenure track (and eleven years prior teaching during graduate school). He has relocated to the desert Southwest and is devoting the rest of his days to reading, viewing, and writing horror of all kinds. He is the creator of Buck Neighkyd (porn star turned occult investigator), Vinnie Dark (PI and studio fixer in 1960's Hollywood), the Stoned Cryptid series from Twisted Dreams Press, and writes horror so far ranging that it boggles the mind. His brand, All the Genres of the Dark, finds everything from quiet horror to screaming volume extreme stuff that got him barred from a tattoo parlor in Indiana (they shoulda read the trigger warnings!). He's the one they warned you about, and is proud to carry that mantle.

~Ken Austin

Ken resides in the picturesque Black Hills of South Dakota with his wife, Penny, and their devoted canine companion, Pobbles. Inspired by the region's rugged landscapes and rich history, Austin has developed a distinguished body of work exploring the genres of horror, mystery, psychological and supernatural fiction. His published works include The Meat Offering, The Red Carnival, Rally of the Damned: The Wendigo Awakens, and Rally of the Damned: The Skinwalker Chronicles, among others. In addition to his horror and psychological fiction, he has also authored the children's book Kylee and Claire-Bear's Enchanted Whispering Woods, a heartfelt tribute to his grandchildren.

~JG Davies-McCabe

JG Davies-McCabe is a nihilist. And likes to present the world in his fiction as such. Grasping and loving hands aren't so much soft and wanting of embrace but rather claws eager for the soft flesh of others. |

Besides all that he has four rats named; cluny, splinter, Rattigan and Zappa. So life isn't all doom and gloom.

~R. A. King

R.A. King is a horror author specializing in psychological horror. A lifelong fan of horror cinema, he also collects books and films. He lives and writes in rural Ohio.

~Sharon Ballentine

Besides being a dedicated writer, Sharon will read almost anything, from historical events to sci/fi to horror to fantasy, but she's too weak of heart to read hardcore "blood and guts" books. She has written the short stories (Choozing) Choosing the (Rite) Right Word and The Jewels of Education, one of which will make the reader laugh out loud, while the other will make the reader cry their eyes out. Sharon has written a novel titled A Look Behind Lightning, book one of which is soon to be released as a comic book series. Sharon loves working with her son and grandson on the comic book series. When not reading, writing, and sketching, she enjoys eating chocolate.

~Stephen Lang

Stephen Lang has harboured a lifetime love of all things terrifying. His short stories and flash fiction have appeared in various collections and anthologies, most recently Year of the Tarot - Wands from Eerie River Publishing, Life and Death from Suspensions Press, Yulehide from Wicked Shadow Press, and online at 101 Words and Dear Booze.

~Thomas Folske

Thomas Folske lives in Minnesota, USA, with his wife, five kids, and three black cats. He loves all things horror, especially 80's horror, gothic and Victorian horror, horror comedy, splatterpunk, and children's horror. He has had over seventy short stories published or in the process of being published, and is currently curating and editing his first anthology.

Find Us!

Find us on Facebook:

https://www.facebook.com/profile.php?id=61555140943354

Instagram: Terror_Monthly

TIkTok: @the_butchered_writers

Also be sure to visit our website to view our shop, find out about upcoming projects, listen to some creepy quickies, explore free stories and subscribe to our newsletters @Thebutcheredwriters.com.

www.ingramcontent.com/pod-product-compliance
Lightning Source LLC
LaVergne TN
LVHW090941080826
845145LV00003B/838

* 9 7 8 1 9 7 1 5 7 9 0 1 6 *